❁❁❁❁❁❁❁❁❁❁❁❁   ❁

One
Dozen
and
❋❋❋❋❋❋❋❋❋❋❋ ❋
One

short stories by
Gladys Taber

J. B. Lippincott Company

Philadelphia ❋ *New York*

For Tay Hohoff ✸

*With a grateful heart for her wit, wisdom,
and patience in and out of book covers.*

Contents

✸✸✸✸✸✸✸✸✸✸✸✸ ✸

Matchmakers

✿✿✿✿✿✿✿✿✿✿✿ ✿

The month after her invalid mother died, Miss Moss took
a small house at the edge of a nearby village. She was
entirely unaccustomed to making decisions, but when she
learned that the new state throughway was going right
through the kitchen, she sold the big house. Even in her
most distracted moments, Miss Moss could not imagine
trucks roaring past her as she made an omelette.

The small house was very old but it looked cozy, somehow. It was quite isolated on a dead-end road, but there
was one neighbor right across the way. The neighbor
was a Mrs. Kowalski, a quiet old lady, said the real-estate
agent. Her husband was dead, her children married and
gone, but she kept on living on the farm because she had
always lived there.

"So there'll be no carryings-on," promised the agent.
Miss Moss said it would be quiet on her side of the

road too. She had never been able to have any friends because her mother was so delicate. The least thing upset her heart.

Miss Moss brought her few belongings to the little house, hung the oil painting of her mother over the narrow white mantel and settled in. She scrubbed and polished and waxed and washed and starched. At noon she had her cup of tea and a boiled egg and maybe half a canned peach. At night she had a bit of lean meat, a dish of peas and a boiled potato. In fact, she ate exactly the same kind of meals she had cooked so many years for her mother.

Her mother had taught her never to trust people, so she was short with the rubbish man and short with the laundryman who came once a week to take her bottom sheet and one pillowcase. He was tall and young and surly, and she felt he resented the smallness of her laundry, but she did most of it herself.

She would have liked to go to the white church in the village, but she never did. She was shy, and she had never been able to leave her mother on Sunday because Sunday was always one of her bad days. So church was never a habit.

When she was sixteen, the year her father died, Miss Moss had a beau. She was slim and small and her hair was soft and light and her wide grave eyes were almost violet. Her beau said so. He kissed her once, in the spring, when they were picking wild violets. Miss Moss kept the violets pressed in a copy of *Jane Eyre*. Regrettably, they stained the pages as they dried. But of course she couldn't go out with him after Father died, for her mother went right into a decline. He went away and married a girl from Iowa and had four children.

Miss Moss paid no attention to the road which wound past her house up to the old abandoned orchard. She seldom looked out the window, for she was so busy. Polish all the teaspoons. Clean the samovar [not that she ever used it, but it was Grandmother's]. Occasionally she would be sweeping the flagstone walk when Mrs. Kowalski came out, carrying a pail. They called good morning. Mrs. Kowalski was a big heavy farmwoman; she walked leaning on a homemade cane; she had her hair tied up in a cloth. She carried the pail to the big red barn and a dozen cats would gather around her. On a warm day, she would sit down on an upturned wooden box and look around her at the yard and the barn and the cats.

Once in a while she would say something to Miss Moss, but nothing ever came of it, for she spoke only Polish.

But one morning Miss Moss opened the back door to toss some tea leaves on a rosebush that might turn out to be alive, and she saw with surprise a big black car coming down the road. It stopped in Mrs. Kowalski's yard and two men in black got out and went in. In a few minutes another car drove up and a man with a bag went in. Miss Moss took her teapot back in and sat right down at the kitchen window where she could see everything. And when she saw the long basket going up the front steps, she knew.

And only yesterday she was in the yard, thought Miss Moss. Oh, dear me. She felt strange and frightened, somehow. She made herself a cup of tea. Her mother's portrait seemed to be glaring at her and she said suddenly, "I shall have tea anytime."

In the next few days life changed on the quiet, dead-end road. Cars came and went. The old lady had a lot of relations, and some of them stayed overnight, for the lights would be on well after midnight if Miss Moss got up to peek.

She was all alone, thought Miss Moss, until she died, and now she has a houseful. I would be glad to help, but of course they don't know me. There should be something. I would like very much to do something for her.

The funeral cars rolled away on the morning of the third day. The house was shut up, curtains drawn. The barn doors were closed and bolted. It was strange how lonely it looked. The house plants had been carried away; two men had collected the cats. There was nothing there, just the blank house, the empty barn.

She had a hard time sleeping that night. Her own house was full of noises, little raps and creaks. Around three, she got up and looked out the bedroom window, pulling aside the ruffled curtains. But there was nobody there; nobody moved.

But it has nothing to do with me, she thought desperately. She took one of the pills the doctor had given her when her mother was dying, and she fell into a thin sleep. But she was tired in the morning.

She walked to the mailbox after breakfast to get the ads that usually came. She never bought anything, but she read about the nylons on sale, the raincoats wholesale priced, the garden tools, and the roses you could get with coupons. She liked the sample breakfast foods that came. It was like having someone send you a gift.

This was a cold morning, and a light snow frosted the old stone fences and the thickets. Miss Moss wore her heavy mittens and her gray wool scarf and buttoned her coat. She got her little bundle and saw that roses were blooming on the top catalogue. She came back down the road, tightening herself against the cold. She looked at her neighbor's yard. And there, by the barn, sat three cats.

One was white and almost full-grown. One was a tortoise-shell with white feet. One was a small kitten, tortoise-shell. They sat and looked at Miss Moss.

"Oh, dear me," said Miss Moss, "they have forgotten three cats! They have gone away and left them behind."

She went into the house and looked at the roses and the ad for the lawn mower. She had toast and gooseberry jam and tea. And then—she couldn't help it—she looked out the back door. The three cats were sitting there with tails wound around them.

They were looking toward her.

They are hungry, she thought; they are hungry. They do not know they are left behind. They do not know where she has gone.

Now Miss Moss faced a real crisis. She could hear her mother's voice quite plainly. Cats are dirty, full of germs. Never get near a cat.

"But they're cold and hungry," said Miss Moss, "and all alone."

By two o'clock she took steps. She heated up a can of evaporated milk and found an old pan and put the milk in it, got on her boots and coat and shawl and went across the road to the barn.

Timidly her voice called, "Kitty—nice kitty. . . ."

The three cats flew toward her, their tails straight up in the air, their paws skimming the snow. The smallest came fastest and first, checked herself about four feet away. The middle cat came just behind, and checked also at a safe distance for escape. The white cat came as if she didn't really care for food but would oblige.

Miss Moss set the pan down and withdrew a few steps.

Instantly the three heads bent; the small tongues flickered in and out; the three tails gradually sank to a relaxed curve.

"They haven't had a bite since she died," said Miss Moss in a whisper.

She went back to her house and washed and ironed and remembered that it was Tuesday and she washed her hair on Tuesdays. All the time she was brushing it and it stood out around her face in a misty cloud, she was not thinking at all of what she was doing. She was thinking how cold that unheated barn must be.

While she had her baked potato and chop, she considered what to do. Everyone needs water, she decided. The brook and pond are frozen solid. Suppose they eat snow?

"But it is certainly not my responsibility," she said firmly, and climbed the steep stairs to her four-poster.

Next day she woke to find a blizzard whirling down from the north. She had plenty of canned goods and plenty of fuel. She was never supposed to go out in what her mother called inclement weather for fear of catching something. But after breakfast she looked out the door for just a moment.

The three cats were sitting under an old truck in the yard, looking over toward her house. Miss Moss reached for her coat and carried the pan of milk out into the snow. The cats met her at the gate and flew ahead of her to the place she had fed them before. There they turned and waited with lifted, expectant faces. They were smart, all right.

They kept their distance until she set the pan down and stepped back, and then how fast the pink tongues flicked in the good rich milk! Once the white one looked around at her. Such a homely cat, but her eyes were aquamarine.

Miss Moss had a harried day. She kept starting one thing and dropping it and beginning things and not ending them, and it was very confusing. She felt that she ought to call the dog warden, who would come and take the little orphans away and—and put them out of their suffering. Yes, this was definitely the course of action.

But who am I, she thought, to take life away from a living creature? What gives me the right? Maybe they'd rather be starving and cold but still just be alive. Who knows?

Miss Moss was quite tired out from all this thinking. But when the snow stopped and the bitter cold dusk settled in, she found herself filling another pan of milk and sallying forth. The snow was deep; it was like walking on white velvet. The three cats heard her the minute the gate latch clicked, and they flew across the road and led her back. The white cat hung behind a little and rubbed against Miss Moss.

"I can't have this going on," said Miss Moss fiercely.

So the next day she went to the village store and asked Mr. Barnes, the grocer, what cats ate.

"Oh, you have cats?" he said cheerfully. "Now, I'll find some scraps of fresh fish, and there are the canned cat foods, and have you plenty of milk? And do you know about rubbing a little bit of butter on their paws now and then?"

"They're wild cats," said Miss Moss, quite overcome.

Mr. Barnes nodded. He was a big man and he leaned on the counter to get on a level with Miss Moss. His bright, Yankee-blue eyes smiled at her.

"Have a gingersnap," he said, holding out the box.

"They were left behind," she said. "They live in the empty barn. They are—they haven't anybody."

"Except you," said Mr. Barnes.

When she got home, she hurried over with her loot, and the three cats simply flew. The littlest one ate so fast she had to stop and hiccup every few minutes. Once she lost her balance and almost fell into the pan. The middle cat looked up at Miss Moss now and then, giving her an inscrutable but rather nice stare. The white cat ate the fastest. Her rather straggly tail twitched.

When Miss Moss got home, she felt very gay. She hummed while she flitted around the house. Her cats were stuffed with food. And she had fresh fish to cook for them tomorrow.

In the morning she went again to the grocery store. Mr. Barnes was sweeping it out, but he put the broom down at once. It was too early for the store to be open, but he was a bachelor and lived just upstairs so he was always around.

Miss Moss drew a deep breath and blushed and spoke right out.

"Mr. Barnes, how does one reassure a cat?"

He leaned on the counter. His eyes twinkled. "Well, now, that is a question," he said. "You take your wild barn cats, they are smart cats. Know their way around.

But if they haven't had a lot of petting and such, they're like deer. You have to treat them like equals."

"Oh," said Miss Moss.

"With dogs, now—" he offered her a candy mint from the glass jar. "With dogs, they'll be anybody's friend. Give a dog one bone, you can't pry him away. But cats mainly always belong to themselves."

"Oh, I see," said Miss Moss. "I never was allowed to have any pets."

It was warm and pleasant in the store, and Miss Moss lingered while Mr. Barnes advised her on varying the diet and putting a bit of butter in the milk. He gave her half a pint of cream; he said it would be sour in a day or so anyway. No charge.

In the course of the next week, Miss Moss had to go to the store pretty often. She always came in with a little rush and said breathlessly, "I can't stay but a minute— I'm terribly busy."

She was, too. The two trips across the road, the waiting while the cats ate, the scrubbing of their pans—well, what with one thing and another, including the four-mile trip to the store, she felt the days flying by like swallows.

Mr. Barnes took to handing her a paper cup of coffee from his thermos, and on a Friday he said, "Well, I've been thinking. I think you ought to name those cats."

"Name them!" Miss Moss turned a very pretty pink. "Oh, Mr. Barnes, they aren't my cats, you see. So I can't really. . . ."

"It would be good to name them," he said. "And as for whose cats they are—well, their former owner seems to have released them."

Miss Moss flew home and got a pad and pencil. The

dictionary was no help. Names such as Theodora, meaning "gift of God," didn't seem to suit. Louise and Grace—or even historical names like Cleopatra and Helen of Troy. . . . No, her cats would not like to be called Helen.

In the middle of her struggle she stopped to feed the nameless ones. It was a pellucid day, the wind diminished for once. The silence of the snow filled the world but a pale sun shone. Miss Moss had a sudden feeling that she and the cats were the only living creatures in the whole universe. She looked over her shoulder at the empty house, and she thought for a moment that one of the curtains had been lifted and let fall, but that was silly.

She bent over and touched the white cat back of her ears. The white cat went on eating. But the littlest one jumped in the air when she felt a hand on her. She did not, however, go away.

At this moment a pair of stray dogs came lounging down the road and sniffed their way right into the yard. They saw the cats; the cats saw them; Miss Moss saw them all at once. And however she did it she couldn't tell, as she said to Mr. Barnes the next day. But she grabbed a big fallen stick and advanced, screaming, at the dogs.

"Go!" she cried, waving the big stick. "Go!"

The dogs trotted docilely away; being farm dogs, they didn't bother with cats much. Miss Moss leaned weakly on the stick until she got her breath. The cats came back from the shelter of the truck and went on with their lapping.

"You might have been killed," said Miss Moss crossly, "and a lot you did about it."

Nevertheless she was flushed with victory. She felt taller and stronger. She watched them lick the pan clean.

The white one was getting fatter very fast. The other two had nice glossy coats now, but they stayed thin.

Tomorrow I shall give you your names, Miss Moss thought.

And then a dreadful thought came to her. The problem of sex entered her life. Possibly they ought to have names like Henry or Gregory instead of . . . and this was something she could not mention to Mr. Barnes.

"I need a cat book," she said over the coffee next morning. "But I should have to go to Waterbury and it is so far and they do drive so fast. . . ."

"Well, what a coincidence," said Mr. Barnes. "It just so happens that I'm going there to do some buying. Suppose you go along with me?"

Miss Moss clasped her hands together. Her mother's warnings about driving with strange men sounded very dimly in her ears. Mr. Barnes was not a strange man and he was also her grocer.

"Is Wednesday suitable for you?" he asked.

"Oh, yes," she said, and ran.

When she got home, she opened the chest in the bedroom and took out the violet wool that she had bought to make a dress for her mother. But her mother had said it was much too bright, so there it was.

Miss Moss cut into it recklessly. She could sew like a French seamstress and once wanted to hang out a sign, but her mother said it was beneath her. Now she made her dress, copying a picture in the mail-order catalogue. It was terribly hard to get the hem even, with no person to speak through pins and say turn, but she kept at it. What's more, from the scraps she devised a tiny wool hat and sewed her best pearl pin on it.

She sat up most of the night, but on Wednesday morning she was up with the chickens, dressed and with Grandmother's amethyst brooch pinned at the neckline of the dress. Then she remembered that she had not fed the cats, so she flew over with the minced poached filets [courtesy of Mr. Barnes].

She and the cats were in the yard when Mr. Barnes drove up in a nice shiny car. He came over slowly, making no noise, and stood beside her.

"Little one eats too fast," he said.

And the little one hiccuped.

Miss Moss had a very odd feeling that now there were five living beings in all this quiet world of snow and ice.

When the cats were finished, she took in the pan and then climbed into the car beside Mr. Barnes. She was shy at first, but pretty soon she found herself telling Mr. Barnes about almost everything. And Mr. Barnes told her how he had to stop school to take care of his parents and how he didn't get to church Sundays because the Sunday papers came in and people just didn't turn up in time for them. Once he had sung in the choir. He would like to again.

He left her at the bookstore and she looked at all the books and finally bought *The Complete Book of Cat Care* by a Dr. Leon Whitney. He sounded authoritative. It said D.V.M. whatever that was. It had two nice cats on the cover, healthy and calm.

And then Mr. Barnes said it was time to eat, so why not? This frightened Miss Moss to death. What to do about paying? Was it immoral to eat with a strange—with Mr. Barnes? How much of a tip did a person leave?

But Mr. Barnes swept her into a German restaurant

where everybody knew him, and the tables had checked covers on them, and it smelled of sauerkraut. This was the downfall of Miss Moss. She cherished a secret passion for sauerkraut, which her mother had never let in the house. She sank into the chair at the little round table and raised her eyes to Mr. Barnes, and said, "Oh—I smell sauerkraut. . . ."

"Hi, Gus," he said. "Double my usual order."

She told the cats about it next day. "I never was so surprised in my life," she confided. "What came with it was delicious, and he said it was ham hocks. Imagine that!" Then she explained to the white one. "I haven't had a meal out in—in years!"

Life was going at a dizzy pace. She still hadn't named them. The book took up a great deal of time, for she was a slow reader. Reading Dickens aloud to her mother had slowed her down; Mother liked every word just so. But when she discovered all the diseases the cats could get, she got faint. She had to hurry down and ask Mr. Barnes if he thought they looked sick.

"They're doing fine," said Mr. Barnes. "Especially the white one. Now drink this coffee, Miss Moss, while I tell you something very private and special."

"What is it?" She looked at him with her eyes wide.

"Your white cat," he said gently, "is, I am sure, going to have some kittens before long."

Miss Moss knocked over the pile of gingersnap packages and turned so pale that Mr. Barnes flew around the counter and supported her. "Don't worry," he said. "It's perfectly usual."

"But the barn—" she cried, clasping her hands, "the barn just with old hay in it. . . ."

"Don't worry," he said. "I think we can manage."

Miss Moss was too distracted to notice his odd use of the word "we." She was worrying about the white cat.

"Now, what I figure," said Mr. Barnes, "is those cats might as well move in with you."

"Move in? With me?"

"Don't you have room?"

"Why—why yes, of course. I have the nice wood range in the kitchen and a corner where a box would go, but—but, Mr. Barnes, they—they are such independent cats!"

"Well, they like you, all right, I could see that. Now, I could come over some night after I close up and help catch them and bring them over. They'd be fine. Just takes a little doing."

Miss Moss said breathlessly, "Oh, would you?" And then she felt her eyes sharp with tears and said, "But they aren't mine. . . ."

"If they aren't yours, they are nobody's," he said brusquely. "Who's kept them alive after the folks forgot them? Who but you? Now let's see, say I drop over sometime tomorrow night. . . ."

A daring idea took forceful possession of Miss Moss.

"Could you—would you—come for supper?"

"Fine," he said. "Just fine."

Miss Moss never had such a busy day. The soups and custards she had cooked for so long would not be right for a big tall man. She knew that. She made up lists, discarded them, made up more.

She knew men liked steak but she might not do it right. She did know how to roast a chicken, and then she decided she ought not to buy the food from Mr. Barnes that he was going to eat, so this involved a trip to the next village. A nice plump chicken she got. "Oh, dear me," she said, "a meal takes so many things." She settled for frozen peas and mashed potatoes with gravy. She could make gravy for anybody. It went like custards.

Dessert. In the early days her mother had liked deep-dish apple pie, and she knew she could handle that. So deep-dish apple pie it was.

She talked it all over with the cats. They were used to her talking to them now, and often listened. But they were not polite. In the middle of her conversation they would bend their heads and start eating again.

"And you have no names," she said, "but Mr. Barnes is going to move you over to my house, and then I will give you names."

She was so tired by the end of that day that she nearly cried. The house was polished like an apple. The best linen was on the table. The chicken was roasting, smelling of herbs and juices. The biscuits were ready to go in the oven.

Suppose he should be late! She sat down weakly when she thought of it.

But he came right on the minute, dressed in his best suit and carrying a box of the store's most expensive candy with a purple ribbon around it.

"Your color," he said, and the reliable Mr. Barnes blushed. "Now," he said, "fix their food and we'll get them."

My, he was a masterful man! Miss Moss fixed the food, trembling a little.

They went out and walked to the neighbor's house, and Miss Moss called the cats.

They came bounding, for it was past their feeding

time. They cast a quick, suspicious glance at Mr. Barnes and then they ate. Meanwhile Mr. Barnes produced a small gunnysack.

"I will put one in," he said, very calmly, "and you hold it. I will put the second one in. You hold it. I put the third one in. Ready?"

Miss Moss was trembling but she felt she had to be ready.

When all heads were bent, Mr. Barnes nipped up the littlest one. There was clawing and scrambling, but he firmly put the kitten in the sack.

"One down," he said.

"Yes," said Miss Moss, shaking.

The next minute he popped the middle one in with a great clamor. The white one came as calmly as if she were ready for the guillotine.

They bore the sack back across the yard. In the warm kitchen Mr. Barnes opened the top and let the cats out. They flew in fifteen directions at once. The littlest one landed on the shelf with the sprigged china; the middle one landed in the sink; the white one landed by the stove and began inspecting the nice box lined with soft blankets.

"Now let's forget them," said Mr. Barnes, "and give them a chance. With a cat you go slowly."

Miss Moss managed to serve the supper. Cats dived in and out around her. But Mr. Barnes gave a person such a feeling of courage. She was pleased that he ate three helpings of everything. He said he never had such a good meal.

They put down a plate of scraps afterward, and the cats came out one by one and devoured them.

"I kind of like the white cat," he said, "although she is a homely cat. But she has spirit."

"They all have," said Miss Moss. "Think of all they've been through. So alone."

"Haven't you been alone too?" asked Mr. Barnes. "I have. I figure everybody's pretty much alone unless they have someone who loves them. Don't you think so?"

Miss Moss just nodded. She didn't know what to say.

"Now, me . . ." said Mr. Barnes, "I always hoped—well, a man thinks about coming home for supper, mowing the lawn, sitting on the porch on a long summer evening. But it's got to be with the right one."

Miss Moss looked down at her clasped hands. "I feel that way too," she said in a very small voice.

"So—so—" said Mr. Barnes, "may I pick you up tomorrow night? It's ham and baked beans at the Grange."

Miss Moss looked right at him. "I'll be ready to leave any time you come," she said.

Mr. Barnes stood up, very tall in the low room. He put out one big brown hand and touched her small one gently.

"Until tomorrow, then," he said. "And don't forget to let our cats out in the morning. They won't run away."

"I do hope they'll be happy here," she said.

He put on his coat and hat, went to the door, and turned to look at her.

"Anybody would be happy," he said, "with you."

When he had gone, Miss Moss put down a last saucer of milk for the cats, who appeared and drank it.

"Cats," she said, "Mr. Barnes and I will name you tomorrow."

Impetuous
Wedding

✦✦✦✦✦✦✦✦✦✦✦✦ ✦

Lucia sat peacefully on the warm sand, getting what would turn out to be a fine sunburn. George was clamming, and she could see his sturdy figure bend and rise with the clam rake. It was the first vacation George had been able to take since Bard, Brad and Burns had taken him into the firm as a partner. And that had been before Jeanie's junior year at Radcliffe.

Three idle, blissful weeks lay ahead. That is, thought Lucia, idle except for scrubbing clams, chopping clams, making clam chowder, simmering clam sauce for spaghetti. George liked clams. But it was vacation anyway. And she wouldn't be cooking for Jeanie's crowd day in, day out—for Jeanie had gone to Blue Hill, Maine, to visit her roommate.

"We'll have a second honeymoon," George had said.

Now he came toward her, leaning with the weight of

the pail. "Honey, you ought to come dig some," he panted.

"Not much use being buried in clams," said Lucia amiably.

She walked along with him to the cottage, her slim legs shedding sand, her face glistening with sun-tan oil. She pulled off her head scarf and shook her dark hair free. She wasn't even going to think of a beauty parlor for three whole weeks!

When they got to the cottage, George set the pail in the shade. "This is the life," he said. "Let's relax and have a drink. Then you can fix the clams while I catch up with the news."

He showered and put on a dreadful pair of too-small faded blue pants and a sweat shirt he must have got from the dump. Lucia took her shower and put on fresh shorts and a pink shirt. Then they sat on the porch of the old-fashioned cottage and sipped frosty drinks.

"It's great to have nothing to worry about," he said.

The phone rang. "Guess it's the Foster man," said George. "I'm going clamming with him tomorrow early."

But when he answered the phone, he raised his voice the way people always do when it is long distance. Lucia set her glass down and went stiff with fear. Jeanie must be sick. Jeanie had an accident. Jeanie was in trouble. Panic turned her bones cold.

George was saying, "Well, well," and then, "You mean it?" and "What do you know?" and "I'll tell your mother. Sure. Sure. Don't worry about a thing." With a final "Well, well," he hung up and came out.

"Now, Lucia, don't get excited. Everything's fine.

Nothing to worry about. All very natural and simple."

"What is it?" Lucia was already in a hospital bending over a bed in which lay Jeanie.

"It was Jeanie," he said. "Now you must be calm. She's old enough, and from what she said I think it is all right."

"What's all right with what?" Lucia was not screaming; it only sounded as if she were.

"She wants to get married a week from Saturday."

"Married?" Lucia's prefectly good drink crashed to the floor. "Are you crazy?"

"Well, that's what she said. She says she will phone back as soon as you have had time to get used to the idea. She says she knows how you react to things. She says I should break it to you gently and then she'll call back. She says. . . ."

"Just because she's involved in a summer romance . . ." said Lucia.

"Well, she can tell you when she calls back." George sat down. "All I know is this is a Jonathan Lewis, just graduated from Harvard and simply the most wonderful. . . ." He sighed. "There goes our vacation."

"Why didn't you tell her it was absurd?"

"Well, I could hardly—well, you know I couldn't really . . ." George finished his drink. "Jeanie is old enough."

By the time Lucia stopped crying it was too late to do the clams. George added cold water to the bucket and dumped in corn meal. "They'll be fine," he said. "We can go to the inn for dinner. Their fried clams are very good."

"I don't want to eat," said Lucia.

The phone rang and she answered it.

"Isn't it wonderful, Mum?" Jeanie said. "I can't wait to see you. And just wait until you meet Jon."

"Now listen, Jeanie," said Lucia, "you cannot rush into marriage on the spur of the moment. It's ridiculous."

"Oh, Mum, I've known him for ages," Jeanie said. "He took me to the Boston Symphony last winter. And then he just happened to come to Blue Hill. . . ."

"Jeanie, just be sensible."

"Oh, I am. I am the most sensible . . . Jon says I am the most sensible girl he ever knew—and Mum, don't worry about a thing. I just want a simple country wedding with the family and Jon's best friends and my roommate. I'm writing you a long letter tonight. We have to get married week after next because Jon has a job in California, and I want to go with him. He's going to hunt Indian relics in his spare time, and I just love Indian relics."

"Spare time from what?"

"Oh, it's some engineering thing—I don't know what. But it's more practical for us to go together. . . . Mum, are you there?"

"I think so," Lucia gasped.

"Well, my letter will explain everything. I've got to hang up now because someone is giving a beach picnic for us."

"Well, I don't think . . ." Lucia began, but the connection was cut off.

Jeanie's letter came the second day. Most of it was an enthusiastic description of Jonathan. At the end she said they had better be married on Saturday in the afternoon, so people who were driving could make it. She and her roommate were going to Boston for the wedding dress that very day, and Mum was not to worry about anything.

Jon would drive her home two days before the wedding. They were getting licenses and stuff in Boston. There might be a few extra guests for the wedding—some Harvard and Radcliffe people, so maybe it would be a good idea to serve something afterward.

Lucia was already packing. "The sooner we get home, the better," she said.

"I don't see what the rush is all about," grumbled George. "I was going clamming. . . ."

"Well, you're not!" she snapped.

"Why can't we just ease in the day before?"

"Ease in? With a wedding?" Lucia's voice rose. "Do you realize I haven't even a dress to wear?"

"Well, can't you wear that flowered thing you wore last summer?"

Lucia gave him a look.

"It's just a simple wedding," he said.

"Well," said Lucia, "it's bad enough to marry a perfect stranger without having your mother wear an old rag."

They drove home with a carton filled with clams bedded in ice. They lived in the country, and as they drove up to the house, Lucia moaned. The man who was to cut the grass had evidently decided that with the family away he needn't bother. The boy who was to paint the picket fence had also laid off, and only a third of the fence shone with fresh white. Two shutters had lost their hinges and slanted against the windows.

"Guess we may as well eat out," said George, lugging in the clams.

"You may eat out," said Lucia, glaring at her favorite man. "I'm busy."

They had fried eggs and toast. And read the letters from Jeanie. She had mailed the wedding dress home. It was a sort of pink. And they had decided to be married in the village church, so would Lucia see about decorating it? There would be a few more people. Jon's favorite professor and wife were coming, and could they be put up for the night?

"But you needn't go to any trouble," said Jeanie.

George went to bed, and Lucia polished the silver. The best lace tablecloth turned out to have a stain in the middle. She put it to soak and phoned Elizabeth, the nearest neighbor. Elizabeth was a farmwoman and had been through many crises. "I'll be over in the morning," she said. "Just don't worry."

The next morning the wedding dress arrived. The postman honked loudly and roused Lucia from her preoccupation with the champagne glasses. Elizabeth was upstairs making up beds.

"We better unpack it and hang it," advised Elizabeth.

They unpacked it. It shimmered like moonlight, delicate with lace and with a foam of veil.

George wandered in, attired in his old army pants and shirt. When he saw the dress he said, "Lucia, we got to go to the city and buy things suitable."

At this point the postman honked again. He had another package. Shell-pink slippers were in it. They looked the size for a fairy. George took one look and said, "Say, hon, you got to get slippers too."

Lucia said savagely, "I have to get a turkey and get it cooked. And see about the church."

"Maybe I ought to fix the cellar door," said George. Lucia told him sharply that he was to go to the market and get everything she had written down on a list.

"Nobody's going down cellar," she snapped.

The phone rang with the firm long-distance peal.

"Mum, there will be seven more coming. But they'll all drive back after. Some of Jon's club friends and a few more of my classmates want to come. It won't be any bother."

Lucia sat holding the receiver until the phone began to buzz. Then she replaced it and went back to the kitchen. Elizabeth was rubbing the spoons. George was banging around aimlessly—quite calm.

When he saw the look on Lucia's face he said, "Now, hon, it's all right. I mean she isn't marrying a gangster or anything. He's even got a job."

"Go down and order the champagne," said Lucia, "and ask Jim to keep it in his cooler so we can pick it up after the ceremony."

"We've got room for a few bottles."

"A few bottles!" she turned fiercely on him. "Do you realize that so far it adds up to forty guests coming to see Jeanie marry this perfect stranger?"

"I thought she only wanted a couple of. . . ."

"I wrote them down. Every time she phones, I add the new ones. While you're out, stop and see if Pam can lend us all her champagne glasses. We have exactly five, two nicked. You and I get the nicked ones and watch yourself so you don't get cut."

Elizabeth said, "Don't worry. It will come out all right. You best finish making up the beds while I run the vacuum and dust."

"Will a case be enough?" George asked timidly.

"If it isn't, they can drink tea," said Lucia.

As she whacked the pillows, she remembered the flowers. She'd call the florist in the next town. She ran downstairs, caught her heel on a step and landed with a crash at the bottom.

"Oh, heavens!" Elizabeth came flying to her. "Are you killed?"

Lucia crawled to her feet. "It wouldn't matter," she choked. Her ankle was not broken, just wrenched, and she limped to the phone. It rang as she reached it. It was long-distance from Jeanie.

"Mum? We'll be home tomorrow. I'm not sure how many yet. I just thought if you'd order the bouquets—there won't be time after we get there—just a cascade for me, corsages for you and Penny, and boutonnieres for Jon and the best man."

"Best man?"

"Jon's roommate, Roger. Jon will pay for them after. . . . Mum, are you there?"

"Yes, I'm here."

"Don't fuss about anything. I thought maybe we could just picnic sort of in the yard."

"Picnic," Lucia said faintly.

"Sure. Carry everything out under the apple trees. To make it easier. Oh, and we're bringing Jon's uncle for the minister. He's a bishop or something. But we called our own minister and asked him to do the prayer and stuff."

"What about his parents?"

"Oh, they can't make it," said Jeanie. "They're in Spain."

Lucia limped back upstairs to make the rest of the beds.

Elizabeth went on vacuuming. It was too bad the good rugs were at the cleaners along with the best slipcovers. Well, nobody would notice much.

They had eggs and bacon again for supper. George was tired of bacon and eggs. In fact, more and more he was beginning to doubt the advisability of the whole procedure. After supper he went out and gloomily threw his precious clams in the swamp. He could see Lucia was in no mood for clams.

The next morning he had to drive Lucia to the nearest sizable city. It wasn't, it seemed, the time of year that Drake's had a good stock of dresses for mothers of brides, especially those which could be worn with no alteration.

"Why don't you just wear that thing you got for the country club banquet last year?" asked George helpfully.

"That old rag? The one I also wore at the Garden Club open house and the reception for the new minister and the concert and Pam's dinner for that lecturer. I'll just go away and not be at the wedding," stated Lucia.

"You look good in anything," said George loyally. "Nobody can hold a candle to you. All you need is to get your hair done. . . ."

"Oh," moaned Lucia, "the beauty parlor! I forgot to call. They'll have to work me in at eight tomorrow morning. They'll have to open up the shop and just work me in."

Eventually she bought a pale lilac silk, which the clerk assured her they would take in while she waited. It wouldn't look at all like a maternity dress when it was snipped in. "And modom can always add her own jewelry."

"Yes," Lucia said to George while they waited, "my dime-store pearls will make any dress."

"Now you know, hon, I was going to get you. . . ."

"We had to use the money for Jeanie's Dartmouth week end." Lucia turned on him suddenly. "What happened to that Dartmouth boy? At least we knew him!"

"He was all right," admitted George, "but he was just another college boy."

"Well, he wasn't a pig in a poke," said Lucia.

"Maybe you might like this one."

"I could wring his neck," Lucia stated flatly. "After what I'm going through."

"Well, after all, Jeanie likes him."

"She's nothing but a baby. He probably looks like a movie star."

On the way home, they stopped at André's. André explained that he could not possibly bake a wedding cake and deliver it to Shadowriver on such short notice. Lucia agreed with him. She knew it was absolutely impossible and she understood perfectly. She would bear up, but she intimated that only one of his wedding cakes would save this affair from being a shambles. André promised the cake. He would bring it himself by noon on Saturday. He'd have to close the shop, but never mind. He didn't normally deliver anything, much less anything that had to go thirty miles. But a wedding without an André cake —he would do it.

By the time they got home, Lucia could barely hobble. Her ankle was swollen until it resembled a rutabaga.

"You ought to go to bed and have a compress on it," said George.

"I've got to bring the dinner plates up from the cellar," she said. "We'll need all those we packed away."

"I'm hungry," said George. "I never knew a wedding meant you starved to death. Let's have a peaceful dinner out tonight—just a good charcoal-broiled steak at Rondo's. Maybe some jumbo shrimp first. And one of those flaming things for dessert."

Lucia shuddered. "How I ever married an insensitive, unfeeling man like you! Here we are about to lose our only—our only daughter to a man we don't even know, and you want to eat!"

"Honey," he said, "look at it this way. You aren't really losing a daughter. . . ."

"But gaining a son," she snapped. "I don't want him. Give him back to Boston, I say. And the bishop, too, and the parents in Spain."

"You've always been a good trouper," said George, "and I know you will be this time too. At least Jeanie didn't sneak off and get married secretly. She wanted to be married at home."

"Home," said Lucia drearily, "looks like the town dump."

"I'll mow the lawn early in the morning and fix the gate," he said.

"You can't paint the house and rebuild the sags in the picket fence and weed the garden," Lucia told him. "Why did we ever go away on that vacation?"

"We didn't know we were going to be summoned back to stage a royal command performance," he pointed out. "It seemed sensible to paint after the worst of the fly season was over, and to get everything cleaned while we were away. It seemed sensible."

"Well," sighed Lucia, "I don't know what all those people will think of a partner in Bard, Brad and Burns who lives in a house with old rugs, broken blinds, leaning fences and a garden of thistles."

"Let's eat out," he insisted, "and get our strength up for D-Day. Maybe Rondo's might even have fried clams!"

There was another thing. Although this was to be a family wedding attended by a few of the bride's and groom's best friends, none of George's and Lucia's friends had been called up and invited. The only guest coming that they knew, therefore, was Penny, Jeanie's roommate, who had been in and out of the house for three years. Was there ever a wedding in which the parents didn't know anybody, not even the groom? It seemed unlikely.

They ate out, and Lucia made lists of the groceries needed. She had certainly stripped the house pending this three weeks' vacation. There wasn't even a scrap in the freezer, because the men were to repair the motor while they were away. Basic supplies consisted of salt, pepper, flour and two cans of tomato soup.

When they went to bed Lucia tried not to keep George awake. But she kept whispering things to herself. She and Elizabeth would do the turkey in the morning; then the man at the market would have to put it in his cooler until the next day. George would have to be sure the church was open for the florist. Would André bring the cake in time? Elizabeth would have to do the salad early.

Then a fatal thought struck her. The groom should not see the bride on the wedding day until the wedding. But in their house the only place one could be unseen was the second bathroom, which had a lock. The groom couldn't just be put away in the bathroom.

She called Pam at eight in the morning. "Don't worry," said Pam. "Just have someone deliver him, and I'll feed him and give him some of those nice pills I got when I was so nervous over Bob's appendix." She added, "You sound hoarse. You aren't coming down with anything, are you?"

"I'm at death's door," said Lucia.

George, groaning and cursing, was mowing the hay which the lawn had become. He had, by now, a healthy hatred of the man causing all this furor. Lucia hadn't been in such a state since the day Jeanie was born. She looked feverish, and her eyes, he thought, were kind of glassy. And her normal sweetness was put down in vinegar.

Lucia gave him an egg sandwich for lunch. He was pretty tired of eggs. Elizabeth and Lucia didn't eat. They were cooking stuff to feed the guests when they came. The kitchen was full of casseroles.

He sat down on the stone terrace and had a cigarette. He was a tired, confused man. Lucia seemed so far away and looked at him as if this were his fault. Maybe she just didn't like men much at this point. Well, he didn't either.

Anyway, Jeanie was too young. What did she know about anything? Marriage could be deadly. Ought to have a year being engaged anyway. By then anything could happen. But Jeanie was impulsive like her mother. Now she was plunging into a dark sea, and he and Lucia hadn't even passed on this man. The whole thing should be called off. He should have put his foot down at that first phone call. But Jeanie's voice trembled with happiness, and he had been kind of knocked off base. This was all his fault—this horrible mistake.

Lucia, dicing onion, had a good excuse to cry. She always bit a piece of bread while dicing onions, but she always cried anyway. Now she mopped the tears away and thought this was all her fault. She was Jeanie's mother. She should have said right away that this was impossible. She should have put her foot down.

"Now I'll finish," said Elizabeth. "You go clean up and fix your face. People get married all the time, and often it works out. And even an unhappy marriage is better than no marriage at all. Women were not meant to be alone."

"I'm just—so scared. . . ." Lucia wept on Elizabeth's cashmere sweater. "I'm so scared."

"Now go put a cold washcloth on your eyes."

Lucia was just pinning back her hair when they came. Her heart raced all over her body, and her bones stiffened. She sloshed some of her Christmas perfume over her and went downstairs.

George came in with Jeanie and Jon. George hadn't changed, and looked like a farm hand. He surely did not resemble a partner of anything. Jeanie flung herself in Lucia's arms.

"It's all so wonderful," she cried in her soft, breathless voice. "Oh, Mum, here he is!"

Lucia's blurred eyes tried to focus on him. Jon was a tall, thin man, like a lot of other men. He had dark hair and blue eyes and a shy smile. There was nothing spectacular about him at all. He did not remotely resemble a movie star.

He had a handclasp worthy of an athlete, however. Her bones ached.

"Everybody else will be along," said Jeanie. "We took the short cut."

She went over and kissed her father. As he looked

down at her, she seemed no older than when she had her first big party.

"Well, hello, Rabbit," he said. Then he got out his handkerchief and blew his nose.

"Gee, I hated to spoil your vacation," said Jeanie. "If it wasn't a matter of life and death, I never would have. You know that, Daddy."

"Oh, well," he said.

"Mum, I hope you put the bishop in the foam-rubber-pillow bed," said Jeanie. "He's allergic to feathers." She laughed. "We put him in another car so we wouldn't get talked to in a sermon sort of way."

"I'll get the bags," said George huskily.

"Jon is to stay at Pam's," Lucia said. "Just bring Jeanie's."

"Let me get them, sir," said Jon.

"No. I always bring them in," said George.

From boarding school, from college, from visits, George had carried Jeanie's bags in. He wasn't going to give this up so fast.

"I've got to go look at the dress," said Jeanie. "Be right back." She skimmed upstairs, as if her feet could hardly be on the steps, so light they were.

Jon and Lucia were left alone.

"You look like Jeanie," he said. "I'd know you anywhere."

"Well, I don't know. . . ."

"This has been pretty rough for you," he said quickly. "I'd have had it different. But this job coming up and all. . . ."

Lucia looked at him. She saw the compassion in his eyes. He was thinking of how she felt.

"Do you love her?" she asked.

"I love her, all right," he answered. "I love her. Believe that."

"She—" said Lucia, "she is—rather special to us."

"She is special to me too."

They looked at each other.

"I know this is right," he said, answering the question in her eyes. "I know. There should have been time for me to win your approval. But being across the continent for a year—well, a year can be a long time." His eyes were honest, his smile shy. "It's kind of like pioneering days."

Before she could speak over the lump in her throat, the house began to fill with the second carload. The confusion was like a carnival. Dishes seemed to fly through the air, coffee cups bounced, silver clattered. Jeanie went off like a sparkler. Finally Jeanie delivered Jon to Pam, the dishes got washed, and uneasy quiet settled.

It began to rain in the night, and poured all day. George took the bishop out for lunch, and the young folks munched sandwiches. André puffed in with the cake. The florist came with the flowers. Somebody brought the champagne glasses, and Elizabeth went to get the turkey from the market cooler. And more guests drove in from Cambridge.

Lucia got the fastener of her dress stuck, and George couldn't find his good studs. And at three-thirty Penny lost one of her contact lenses. Everybody went around like truffle hounds while Penny wept. Someone found it under the bed.

Pam sent over a raincoat with a hood for the bride. And at four-fifteen the guests filed into the little village church, the organ began to play, and Jeanie came down the aisle on George's arm. She looked like moon mist and apple blossoms. When she and Jon looked at each other, the church seemed filled with light.

Afterward George had to try to get Lucia's left slipper back on. It was a mistake to take it off, because her ankle had swelled more.

There was a slight delay because one car wouldn't start, and the bishop tucked up his robe and hopped out in a puddle and gave it a manly push. The picnic under the apple trees had long since been abandoned, and the buffet was served at the dining table. Champagne corks popped all over. George cut his lip on his cracked glass.

Jeanie and Lucia had to go to the back entryway to have a few words. Jon was lugging the suitcases to the front porch.

"Oh, Mum, it was simply perfect," said Jeanie. "It was just perfect. And isn't Jon the most wonderful—the most perfect . . . and oh, Mum!" Then they cried together as mothers and daughters must.

"And you know, Mum, you aren't losing a daughter. . . ."

"I know." Lucia wiped her eyes. "I'm gaining a son."

"And I told you not to worry," Jeanie mopped her face. "I just wouldn't have wanted a thing different. I just wanted a simple country wedding with the family and a couple of our best friends from college."

Lucia choked. Then Jon looked in anxiously. "I think we ought to get started," he said.

They were off in a flurry of confetti, and gradually the guests sorted out their rubbers—one was never found —and matched the right umbrellas to the right person, almost, and they went too. The bishop gave Lucia a warm handclasp. "Let not your heart be troubled," he said, half smiling. "This is right for them both."

Elizabeth left last, promising to come and help clean up in the morning. "Don't touch a thing," she said.

Lucia sank onto the sofa, and George took off his coat and tie. He came over and kissed her and she clung to him. He ruffled her hair. "They're in love," he said, "and there's nothing to worry about."

"I think so too." Lucia rested her head against his starched shirt.

"But right now," observed George, "I'm thankful we had only one son to gain!"

Honey and
the Home Front

❀❀❀❀❀❀❀❀❀❀❀❀❀ ❀

It was a beautiful morning, clear and gay as a trumpet note. The year was 1945. The golden light of spring fell on the five cocker puppies, tumbling in the new grass around their mother's golden ears. Honey herself turned a very chill shoulder on them; they had begun to bore her. Eight weeks was long enough to feed and wash and train five children, she felt.

The puppies felt wonderful. Teddy had given them a bath the day before; they shone like animated satin. Their ears were light and clean as kites flying in the spring air. The two black boys couldn't keep up with the three girls; they panted heavily behind, pink-flannel tongues lolling.

Honey removed herself to the porch swing, closed her dark amber eyes, and rested her paws. But Jessica was coming out the back door to do some spring planting, and the puppies flew after her, hey-nonny-nonny-oh. Jessica wore her sailing-blue-slacks and a torn sweater, and her tawny hair tied in an old scarf. Her knees ached. Sometimes she felt that being mother and caretaker and household help and man of the family was a pretty heavy load. But Jerry wasn't here to put in the garden; Jerry was somewhere in the Pacific. Jerry hadn't seen his daughter in the college play, lovely and proud. Nor Teddy in the high-school swimming meet. Nor the puppies opening their milk-blue eyes on this strange world.

Jessica spoke aloud suddenly, "Darling, I'm afraid! I'm not coping very well. I do need you home."

Daffodil sped away with the early Crosby beets. Sonnet had the trowel. Jessica chased them away, but Sonnet came back to be kissed, just to be certain things were all right. She was like a small round piece of moonlight.

Bombardier and Pilot, the black boys, began to dig beside her. Dirt fanned up behind their fat little rears.

"Look, dears," said Jessica, "you aren't really helping the food front." She pushed her sleeves up. *Where am I going to get the money for all those extra bills?* she worried. *I never was very good at figures*. She took the edible podded peas away from Jonquil and spaded the ground for them fiercely. Four hundred dollars due on the college bill—and you couldn't ask a college to wait. Insurance premiums due. . . . The plumbing bill. . . .

Beulah came out with the wash, and the puppies fell on the basket joyfully. "Hey, you gemmun, fotch back them pins!" she called. "Closepins is scarce." She flew across the lawn like a large, heeling sailboat.

"I'll lure them in," said Jessica, taking off her muddy gloves.

Convoyed by five, she went in. They loved to swing on the cuffs of her slacks. She might as well face that desk anyway, and finish the spading later. *I can't sell a War Bond*, she thought dismally. *Jerry would never speak to me if I came to that.*

Honey followed her and sat on the sofa, and her children assailed the slip cover fiercely. Jonquil kept flinging herself up and plopping back. Her stomach was as plump as a butternut, and hampered her in leaping.

The checkbook stub showed nine dollars and sixty-three cents. If her figures were at all wrong, she'd be overdrawn. And she had little faith in her adding.

She added and subtracted and sorted bills endlessly, but she couldn't seem to come out even. By the time she pushed back her hair over an aching forehead and went to the window to look out, it was late enough for Teddy to be riding down Linden Street on his bicycle. He was thin, she thought, but growing so tall, and looking more like Jerry every day. It made her heart contract to see the way he held his head and looked out of those gray eyes. Ann was drifting up the walk, too, her burnished hair taking all the sun.

"I," said Jessica to Bombardier, "need a husband to keep on hand. All the time, and especially now."

Teddy whistled and all the cockers flew. They pushed open the screen door and made a lovely cascade down the steps. Teddy and Ann sat on the grass, and there was much laughter and growling and tugging. In the lovely spring light, the children and cockers looked like youth and joy incarnate. Jessica brushed mist from her eyelashes.

Beulah stuck her head out of the dining-room window and called, "You come in and wash up, both you! We got Eyetalian spaghetti and lemon bisque for supper!"

"Oh, Beulah, my figure!" moaned Ann.

"Your figger! Got to look twice to see is you there," laughed Beulah. . . . "And, Teddy, you shut up the puppies while we eat. I jes step off one and on other; they like greased runners on a icy hill."

At supper, Jessica sat at Jerry's place, with Honey at her feet. The puppies, shut in the study, were busy taking things to pieces.

"Children," said Jessica, as she served the spaghetti, "I've been thinking. We ought really to—to find homes for three of the puppies."

"What for?" Teddy looked horrified.

"Well, after all, we only planned to keep one. You know we bred Honey to that champion stud dog just to have the fun of raising one nice litter and have one to keep, so we would have two dogs."

"Five is just as easy as two," said Teddy, his eyes very large. His voice cracked.

"It isn't entirely that," said Jessica desperately, "but it is pretty expensive and—and we aren't coming out very well with the money this month. The allotment money hasn't come. . . ."

Ann said, "Moth, you mean we're hard up?"

"Well," said Jessica weakly, "we have nine dollars and sixty-three cents in the checking account."

"And my college bill due!" Ann went white.

"Now, I don't mean to worry you," said Jessica hastily. "I was only trying to plan—I mean, it seems the sane, reasonable thing to do—to sort of cut down. Your father wouldn't want us to sell any bonds. . . ."

"You can't sell a War Bond!" Teddy said. "That sabotages national defense." His freckles stood out sharply when he got white. "Mom, what you really thought was we ought to sell three of them, isn't it?"

"Five is really too many to keep," explained Jessica, feeling worse by the minute, "and I only wondered. . . . They are champion stock and we thought at first. . . . But let's just think it over anyway."

Ann said, "I suppose it seems as if a family wouldn't really need six cockers."

Nobody ate the lemon bisque. They left the table in silence, and Teddy went directly to the study. Jessica moved wearily back to the desk, and Ann took her psych books upstairs. Jessica heard Teddy climbing the stairs with Pilot. Presently he came down with him, and went back up with Bombardier. Jessica listened. He made five trips, up and down, a puppy in his arms each time. Her heart ached. He was trying to see which puppies he could best part with, that was evident. Teddy's whole heart was involved with those puppies; he had dreams of showing them, winning prizes.

If she could only get through this one month, maybe it would be better. She slammed the desk top as Teddy came in with Bombardier.

"Looky, Mom," he said. He put the puppy down, lifted his hand and said firmly, "Hup!"

The puppy spanked himself down so hard there was a solid thump. His tail went mad with excitement.

"He hups already," said Teddy proudly. "I wanted to ask you, Mom, is he smarter than Pilot 'cause he hups or is Pilot smarter because he retrieves a ball? Which do you think?" His troubled, earnest eyes besought her.

"Oh, dear me, I don't know," said Jessica. "Darling, they are your own puppies, and if you can't bear to part with any of them—well, I am not going to make you!"

Teddy looked away. He spoke gruffly, "I put my pig bank on your dresser. I got eighteen dollars in it. I thought you could use it." He gathered up the puppy and moved away.

Jessica's eyes were misty again. That was his bond money, saved diligently; it was all he had in the world. Well, she thought drearily, she could go to the bank in the morning and talk to Mr. Morse and see what to do.

But in the morning she had an early phone call from Jerry's mother in Abbotsville. She was laid up with a sprained ankle, and could Jess come over and help out a few days? In an hour Jessica was on the bus, Beulah having promised to come and look out for things until she got back.

"A good thing," she said. "Give me a chance to turn out your room and clean it good."

Teddy watched his mother go off, and then went to the kitchen. He had Jonquil tucked under his chin. His face was white and set.

"You ain't getting a sick spell?" asked Beulah, eyeing him.

"No. Beulah, Mom is really in a jam for some money, isn't she?"

"Reckon so. A woman can't handle things like a man. This house purely does need a husband. A house with no man. . . ."

Teddy stood up very tall. "I'm the man," he said with

dignity. "I guess I can take care of things while Pop's gone."

"What you studyin' to do?"

"I—I'm going to sell three of the puppies," he said, his voice suddenly husky; "now, while Mom's gone."

Beulah stared, then rocked back on her heels. "How you going to do that?"

"I'm going to put an ad in the paper," he said. "They're pedigreed A.K.C. registered puppies. I ought to get a lot, but I'm going to ask only fifty, on account of it's war-time."

"Oh, me, oh, my!" said Beulah. "You stand there and tell me anyone going to pay fifty dollars for something to chew up house and home? Go away from me."

"They will, though," Teddy spoke shakily. "Ours are —are pretty special puppies. Now, you take Bombardier; he's . . ."

Beulah turned on him. "Now looka here, Teddy, you ain't figuring on selling my li'l black man? You don't dare take him out of this house! He's going to be Beulah's big old hunter man."

"But I guess Pilot has a better front," said Teddy doubtfully.

"Front!" Beulah spoke scornfully. "Ne'mine front. That Bombardier is smarter than a insurance man. Don't talk to me about selling him!" She bent over the dishpan and made a great clatter with silver. "And you leave that small Sonnet too."

"Gosh, Beulah; she's the runt of the litter!"

"So was Napoleon a runt," said Beulah darkly.

Teddy went out hastily. The day was long. He spent the afternoon painting his bike; painting very slowly, but getting paint in his hair and on his clothes and all over the garage. Then he sat on the back porch with his chin resting on one stained hand. Honey snuggled against him, watching him with dreamy amber eyes. His free hand moved over her velvet nose.

"We had a lot of fun," he said slowly. "Five is an— an awful good number to have around. Now take that Jonquil, she's gonna look just like you, and be awful smart too. You take Daffodil, she's got it. It."

Honey kissed his thin wrist. Her long ears swept over his arm.

"We'll be kind of alone," he said. "You got to tell yourself, Honey, it's your bit for the war. You keep on telling yourself that, like I am. You see, now this is the front, too, in a way." He swallowed, and blinked back hot tears.

Beulah opened the door and held out Pilot. "You sell him you got to ask five dollars more," she said; "he's done et up all the blue points off your ration book."

Teddy collected all the puppies in his room and played with them a while. Then he cleaned up, took a last look at them, and went out, walking as fast as he could down Main Street to the *Bee* Office.

He made up a swell ad. "Cockers for sale," it read. "Pedigreed, intelligent, beautiful, specially trained by hand, very lovely. A.K.C. registered. Call Teddy Ainslee, Linden 459. Priced fifty dollars and up." He was doubtful about the "and up," but most ads said that in the *Dog News*. He paid for the ad and went home, dragging his feet.

If he had a good job, he could get money. But a fellow couldn't take down storm windows and mow lawns and clean furnaces fast enough to make that much money. Even if he quit the team and the band and worked all that time.

Maybe nobody would buy one. He'd have them. But still and all, he had to take care of the family. It was up to him strictly. He got one of his stomach upsets worrying, and Beulah put him to bed early.

And Saturday morning the phone rang while he was brushing and posing Jonquil.

He took the call and rushed out to Beulah. She was just at the most delicate point in her light rolls, but she stopped when she saw his stricken face, the freckles standing out like cinnamon drops on a white cake icing.

"Your grandma's leg broke?"

"It's a man," gulped Teddy, "wants a black male! Delivered today for a birthday present. He—he never even waited to come look at him! He says he's leaving for New York—it's Mr. Greyson, the factory owner. I—I said the blacks were sixty, and he said he'd have the check in the afternoon mail!" Teddy sat down suddenly, getting that green tinge around his mouth.

Beulah threw down the dough. Her wise dark eyes studied him a moment, and then she said, "Teddy, you is actually the man of the family! No argument about it. Imagine you making that money for your mother."

"Yup," Teddy's head hung down.

"She's going to be mighty proud of you," said Beulah firmly; "she say you take after your father."

Teddy's head lifted a little.

"And now I'm going to make you a devil's-food cake for supper," she said, "and you can ask the boys over tonight to play that crazy wild card game, and you can have popcorn and cocoa."

"Gee, Beulah, thanks." He almost smiled. "I—my bike isn't dry. How'll I get him across town?"

This was a faint loophole, and they both knew it.

"I'll run up attic and find you a craton," she said. She always called them "cratons." "You can ride the bus with a craton."

"He won't like it," predicted Teddy.

" 'Twon't take but half an hour. I'll find a nice big craton."

Teddy went to the study, where Honey had tucked the children up in their packing box. Five happy faces lifted instantly. Teddy knelt and laid his hands on the two black males. They both scrabbled and hopped, tails agitated, ears flying. Their eyes shone; damp rubber noses pushed against his hot fists. Teddy gathered them up with a strangled cry. Pop was so far away. Mom was gone too. Nobody could help him now. He hugged the warm fat bodies against his thin chest.

It took money to live, to get along. Money didn't just grow out of the ground. It had to come with struggle. It was hard—lots of things were hard, he'd found out. But a guy had to be a man. A guy had to take it. He closed his eyes, dropped one puppy back and ran with the other. But he knew he had Pilot by the way his ear was being chewed lovingly.

The house across town was big and elegant in a cold sort of way. Teddy rang timidly and the door was finally opened by a butler.

The butler made him nervous. Teddy evidently made the butler nervous, too, for he backed away hastily.

"I got a birthday present," said Teddy hoarsely, "from Mr. Greyson. He's not happy in this carton is why he's yelling."

The butler gave a faint sound, then ushered Teddy into the big drawing room. He would call Mrs. Greyson, he said, still speaking faintly.

Teddy opened the top and Pilot whisked out. Mad with joy, he rushed wildly for Teddy, darted around and around him, flew across the pale fawn-colored carpet and then, overcome with emotion and excitement, made a large puddle over a clump of roses.

Just at this moment a tall severe woman came in, wearing a lacy gown and looking rather like pictures of Queen Mary, only not so kind.

She said, "Oh, my Aubusson! Little boy, is this supposed to be a gift for me?" Her voice was colder than ice skates, and Pilot began to tremble.

"Yes'm," said Teddy; "this is Pilot, my—your puppy."

"Ridiculous," she sniffed, sweeping her skirt aside. "I didn't want a puppy in the first place! And one this size— not even housebroken! Well, he can go in the garage, I suppose."

Teddy and Pilot kept backing away together, and Pilot sat down finally on Teddy's foot. His frightened eyes were lifted to Teddy.

"You mean stay in a garage?" asked Teddy slowly.

"I don't expect to have him ruining my priceless antiques in the house," she said, "no matter what quixotic idea George had in buying the creature."

"But he's always lived in our house!" Teddy's voice trembled. "He's a house dog!"

"He doesn't act it!"

"He's nervous," said Teddy.

She took a step forward. Pilot was definitely getting a neurosis, and he flew across the room like a small fat bunny. And pulled a light cord. A large lamp with sort of green figures toppled from the shiny piano and made a loud crash. The woman's face turned livid, but before she could raise her hand, Teddy had the puppy inside his shirt.

"Ma'am," he said, and frightened as he was, he looked at her steadily, "I think there has been a mistake. This puppy is not for sale. I—I will send back the check."

She was choking. "Of all the notions—of all the ridiculous. . . ."

Teddy flew. The butler opened the door quickly, and bent over and whispered, "You oughtn't have left the little thing here anyway. She's a—a terrible woman. That's why her son won't live with her."

The carton was left behind in the flight, so Teddy and Pilot had to hike home, mile after mile. And there was the check waiting, when Teddy limped in. He held it in his hands, a check made out to him for sixty whole dollars. The price of Pilot's happiness. Slowly, he sat down and wrote the note: "I could not leave my puppy as she does not like little dogs."

After supper he went out and mailed it. As he came back, a car drove up in front of the house, and a woman with a sweet face got out and looked doubtfully at him.

"Is this the place where there is a puppy for sale? We're looking for a cocker. A female. For my little girl."

"Well," said Teddy reluctantly—"well, I did have. . . ."

"Oh, may we come in, then? If you'll help Joan . . ." She gestured toward the car.

A small, pale, twisted little girl was propped on pillows inside. She had so much steel and leather around her legs that Teddy could hardly get near her. But he helped the lady lift her out. They got into the house and met Honey in the hall.

"Oh, Mother! Oh, the lovely, the beautiful! I want her!" Joan's face was radiant.

Honey gave her a long thoughtful look, moved over and kissed her slender hand.

"But it's the puppies we must look at," said her mother.

Teddy opened the study door. Joan held out her hands. "Oh—oh! May I touch the middle one? Just touch her?"

Daffodil snuggled, enjoyed the kissing immensely. "This is the one, Mother! This one!"

Teddy scuffed the rug with his toe.

"Will you sell her? I'll make her happy! I promise!"

"Aw, sure," said Teddy, looking away. "Sure, you take her."

Daffodil rode away, wrapped in Joan's pink sweater. Teddy had the check. It was fine, just fine. So he took one look at the four left, and went upstairs and cried. Honey got in his lap and lapped away the tears.

"But we had to do it!" he said in a choked voice. "Gosh whiz, we had to!"

Monday morning he went down to cash his check with the other businessmen. He met the family dentist, Doctor Brown, and tried to duck, because Doctor Brown had a way of dragging a guy in to get his teeth cleaned. But Doctor Brown chased him and caught him, and it seemed he had read the ad in the paper. Dick Brown was coming home, wounded, from Germany, and Teddy had better get the puppy over right away. Teddy agreed soberly. My, you could make a lot of money selling dogs, if you liked to sell dogs.

He found Beulah in what she called a snit. "Every time

I get on my knees varnishing your mother's floor, I got to run down and answer the phone," she said. "You got dozens people want the puppies; you call them back."

"I'm not going to sell one, unless to someone I like," he said. "And anyway I don't feel so good; I guess I got a cold. If a person came here, they might catch something. They better not come."

"You better go to bed."

"I got to deliver a puppy to Doctor Brown."

Beulah laughed. "Man, there's one dog will have clean teeth!"

The phone rang.

"I'm gone," said Beulah hastily, retreating.

Teddy admitted under pressure that he did put an ad in the paper. Yes, he had a blond female puppy, but— well, she was awful small and prob'ly if they looked around. . . .

It was no use. A Mrs. Cartwright was coming at eight for the puppy. She said her own darling Bittsy had died last week because she was eighteen years old, and she had said she was never going to have another dog, but she couldn't bear it, and she was absolutely crazy looking at Bittsy's empty bed and her leash, and it wasn't being disloyal to Bittsy's memory, but the house was so dreadful with just herself and two parrots and the three cats.

In the end, Central cut in and said in a frosty voice, "Will you limut your call to five minutes, pullease?"

"And she can have all my meat points," finished Mrs. Cartwright firmly. "I have to eat rabbit food myself."

"But honest . . ." protested Teddy faintly.

"No, I don't need to hear any more. I love her already. I feel it. I always feel things."

Teddy replaced the receiver and turned to Honey, who was not too old and settled to chew the phone cord.

"Honey," he said sorrowfully, "we're going to be lucky if you and I get out of this without being sold ourselves. Gosh, whoever said it was hard to sell things?"

Beulah creaked down the stairs. "It's the war," she said. "People got money, some people, and you can't buy much any good hardly. Even the clo'es is made mostly of sympathetic materials. They fall to pieces the first time you get in them."

The phone was ringing again. Teddy felt confused. Too much was coming on him too fast. He had practically a fortune in his pants pocket, he felt, and still money didn't seem to make a guy feel so wonderful. Money, he thought morosely, isn't everything.

"Hello," he said thickly. "Who's it?"

"This is Craig Duncan," said a cheerful voice, "of Duncan and Duncan. I need a puppy by tomorrow morning. In fact, I've got to have one!"

"But I don't think. . . ."

"Isn't this the man who has puppies to sell?"

"Well, I really—well, as a matter of fact, these puppies. . . ."

"So you are the one! Now, your ad said A.K.C. registered. Right?"

"Right," said Teddy.

"What's the breeding? Not too good, I suppose."

Pride rose. "Best there is, sir. Champion Rees Bombardier and Heartsease Honey."

"Sold," said the voice happily; "and what a break for me! Look, I'm shipping out tomorrow, and my girl feels kind of upset, and I thought a nice puppy—something to keep the memory green, you see. I'll drop by and pick her up. Red or black, but a female. I want a female."

"But listen here, Mr. Craig Duncan. . . ."

"I'll bring a basket." The phone went dead. Honey had finally worked through the insulation.

Teddy rushed out to Beulah, who was getting supper.

"Your sister's spending the night at the sorority house," she said. "I'm fixing you and me a snack out here."

"What'll I do, Beulah?" He sat down. "Look, Beulah, two people bought Sonnet! They're both coming to get her! I couldn't seem to get them to even listen to me!"

"Heavenly day," said Beulah. She sat down and stared at him with sympathy. "All you gets into is trouble. One those buyers going to be awful mad."

Teddy twisted his feet around the chair legs. "I can't help it!" He spoke desperately. "They wouldn't let me say anything at all! Look, I'm gonna deliver Doctor Brown's puppy right off, before I get him taken twice. You just wait supper!"

Troubled and unhappy, he trudged down the street. He had Bombardier in his arms. Pilot he just couldn't put through anything more. What would he do? He just couldn't sell all the females, but how could he sell Sonnet twice? He was in a jam all right. When he left the Browns' he was numb with misery. It was such a lovely pale clear evening, sweet with spring, but he didn't feel like spring at all. Jonquil would have to go; he might as well face it. Unless—he might get out of it by jacking the price up to sixty for one customer. But which one needed a puppy worst? Well, better let the first one take Sonnet.

He walked slower and slower, turning the corner and moving past the Peale house. Mr. Peale was out on the front walk with the Peale cocker. Teddy stopped and looked her over carefully. She was straining at her leash.

"She won't leave her pups," explained Mr. Peale. "I have to drag her away. I never saw such a dog—overconscientious."

"Could I see the puppies?"

"Sure, come around back. They're in the kitchen."

Teddy knelt and looked at the babies. They were particolors like their mother, black satin and white silk; they were seven and a half weeks old, and one stood up and barked like a man dog. Their eyes were still darkly blue. They waved their paws in the air when they fell over one another.

"Gosh whiz," said Teddy, "they look very O.K. One thing we never did have was a particolor." He picked up a fat puppy and automatically smoothed the soft nose. "You can't hardly find anything like a good pup," he said.

Much later that night, Jessica Ainslee came home. She had tried to phone, but the line seemed to be out of order, so she had to walk from the bus, carrying her bag. The first thing she saw was a letter from Jerry propped on the table. She flew to the living room and opened it. He was safe! He was well! He was busy! He was worrying about her. This was the time of year they usually ran short, he said. And he didn't trust her head for figures. He just wanted to remind her to cut the coupons from those bonds in the safety-deposit box. There should be about five hundred there, and if she didn't need it, she could buy War Bonds with it. It was a miracle! A miracle his remembering how she would forget those coupons! Jerry wasn't actually so far; he was there with her!

She heard Honey scratching at the study door, and she ran to open it before she took off her things. Honey gave her a distracted look and rushed wildly away. What in the world was the matter with her? Jessica stared after her. Then she snapped on the study light, and then she gave a slight scream.

"Hey, Mom! Mom, is that you?" Teddy's voice sounded from the upper hall. "Mom, you home?"

"Teddy Ainslee, come right down here!" She was still staring at the packing box.

"I'm coming!" He fell down three steps, made the rest in a gallop. "Mom, I got a surprise for you!"

"Surprise!" Jessica was pointing at the puppy box.

Pilot was hanging half out of the box, climbing valiantly over three strange black-and-white puppies, smaller than Honey's but very, very lively.

"Where did these come from?" demanded Jessica.

Teddy said, "I bought them!"

"Bought them?" she asked faintly. "Bought three puppies?"

"It's perfectly simple," he assured her. "Mr. Peale wanted to sell them; it was a real bargain. You'd hardly ever get such a real bargain in your whole life, Mom. You see, they're just right to nick in with our blood lines. . . ."

"Teddy!" she gasped. "You bought three more puppies?"

"Well," he said, "after I sold three, it was—it was kind of lonesome for me and Honey."

"Sold three?" Her head was whirling. She stared at her son.

"Yup. I sold one twice," he admitted. "The lady had just lost Bittsy and the man was shipping out, and they bought Sonnet, but it worked out when they talked it over." He said, "The new male is pretty nice too."

She sank down on the sofa and put her hand to her head. "You sold three puppies and bought three more?"

"That's what I'm telling you. It's the surprise."

"It's a surprise all right," she said faintly.

"You needed the money," he said, "and I put it all in your glove box. The profit, I mean."

"Profit?"

"Mr. Peale gave me a bargain, on account of I took all three in a clump," he said, "so I paid twenty-five apiece for them. So I got a profit of eighty-five dollars all told. And I still have the stock." He eyed her anxiously. "You see now? I sold ours like I was supposed to, and it's all right, isn't it? The only thing is, Honey can't dope it out. She like to have taken the skin off the new ones washing them. She seems kind of nervously upset."

"I don't wonder," said Jessica. "It would upset anybody."

"Will eighty-five be enough for you?" he asked.

He reached down and gathered Pilot in his arms. The biggest particolor rose and braced his fat legs four-square and uttered a fierce woof.

Teddy eyed him fondly. "I'm gonna train him good. He's smart. I'm gonna name him after General Patton." He hesitated. "You think I ought to have kept all the money for you?"

She opened her lips to tell him she didn't need any of it. And then she closed them again. "Teddy," she said finally, "I think you used unusual judgment. And when I say 'unusual,' I mean it. Your father will be very proud of you. He'll feel the family is in good hands."

Teddy's eyes shone. He stood straighter. He looked at her with so much of Jerry's look that she swallowed the lump in her throat. She'd lay that money aside, marked for Teddy's kennel. But this wasn't the time to say so. This was the time to be proud and grateful for his taking the responsibility for the family at such a cost.

They went out to the kitchen for some hot cocoa and sandwiches. Honey was hiding under the stove, but she was lured out with a molasses cooky, her favorite kind.

"You'll get over the shock," Jessica told her. "Mothers often have shocks to get over."

Teddy stood close to her, and just happened to lean against her a moment. "Gosh whiz," he said, with a small sigh, "I'm glad you came home, Mom. I had kind of a hard time."

Jessica held him tightly a moment. "Yes," she said, "I know how it is. Growing up is about the hardest thing there is."

Dear Bachelor

✺✺✺✺✺✺✺✺✺✺✺✺   ✺

Spice Hill, August 10

Dear George:

I'm sorry the measles prevented me from coming in to the play. I hope Ruth Bell could go with you on such short notice.

George, I didn't mean to be cruel about you being just a self-sufficient bachelor, really I didn't. All I mean is that here I am with Roger and Barbie and the baby and they are my job, especially since their father is gone, and things just keep happening. If you want to get married, you should start from scratch, I mean, with a nice free unattached female—like Ruth Bell. That was all I meant.

I do hope Roger thanked you for the wonderful archery set, it was so thoughtful.

Lucia

Happy Adventure Camp, Sundy

Dear Uncle George:

The bow and arrows came. I knocked out the mess-hall window. Mom says Barbie's got measles. I hope this finds you the same. Ha! Ha!

Roger

Mondy

Dear Uncle George:

I et the whole box. It was good, the chewy best. My spots are going.

Barbie

Spice Hill, August 14

Dear George:

The concert sounds lovely and I would love to come in and go but the only baby sitter I could find hasn't had measles. Barbie's upset stomach from eating all the candy while I dashed down for groceries is all right now.

Are you sure you had measles when you were a boy? Otherwise I do *not think* you should try to come out Friday night. Barbie keeps asking when you are coming and I just tell her she will have to be patient.

Lucia

Dear Uncle George:

They make us write letters onct a week. I wrote to Mom but altho you are not a real relation, I said I would write my Uncle George since I call you Uncle if you arnt.

I can make the canoe go by bouncing up and down, no paddles. Duff got in a bees nest, boy he looks neat!

Knock, knock, whose there? Tarzan. Tarzan who? Tarzan stripes forever. It figures.

Roger

Dear George:

On account of the measles, would you be able to meet Roger at Grand Central and take him across to the Penn Station for the 5 o'clock train? I hate to bother you but I just don't like him to be alone in the Big City.

It was sweet of you to send Barbie the crayon set. She drew the most fascinating figures all over the bedroom wall, giraffes and elephants. I feel she may have talent. But I have to repaper.

Lucia

Dear, dear George:

I feel terribly that you had such an awful time with Roger. I do apologize and I know you can see now why I can't marry you. My children are just too difficult.

Of course he does have a lot of imagination and a great deal of spirit and he is fundamentally sweet and darling.

You should have taken the bow and arrows away from him before you ever got in the taxi. A small boy on the way home from summer camp is a pretty wild proposition at best. And then he must have been startled when he leaned out of the taxi window and shot off the arrow and it just happened to hit a policeman. Of course when the officer loomed up, all he could think of was to say you were kidnapping him and he was merely trying to get the officer's attention to be saved. Actually, I think it shows an ability to meet situations, don't you? But

I can imagine how you felt being dragged to the station when the officer wouldn't believe you, who you were and all.

And I do not think the officer should have agreed with you that if Roger's story was made up, both of you should paddle him. All the modern books say . . . but never mind that.

Honestly, George, when Roger got off that train, lugging that huge bow and arrow set and the jar of canned frogs, and so peeled with sunburn—I was just thankful he was back. You probably wouldn't have felt that way at the moment, when you were just through phoning the office and everything about your not turning up.

And I am so sorry, too, that Roger got lost at Radio City. You must have felt awful when you looked in the next seat and found he was not there any longer. I do think the management was wonderful to page him and announcing it from the stage was a very fine idea too. I may candidly say I would have been in hysteria at that point. Roger is so little, really, and so trusting. He might go off with anybody who had enough bubble gum.

And I do think he was clever when he couldn't find his way back from the men's room—he says you weren't in the same place when he went back—and he was brave just to stand by the main lobby outside, figuring you would have to come out some day.

I know you are thankful to have one small boy returned home and not loose around New York with a jar of frogs and a bow and arrow set while you were trying to locate him.

> Gratefully,
> Lucia

Spice Hill, Monday night

Dear George:

I got to thinking in the night last night after you left and I just don't want you to think I don't feel you are about the very nicest—and the most thoughtful—I mean since Roger senior left us. But I think a woman with three children is too much, as I have said—and no matter what you say about my eyes and my smile and all, I still have three children. It's what I would myself call a matrimonial hazard of the first water. Or a five-alarm fire.

But I have the brown orchid that you say is like my eyes right by the bed.

But George, do you think that baby sitter has a steady, sane look in her eyes? I just read of the most awful thing —a baby sitter flung a baby out of the window! I think next Saturday I better stay home.

Lucia

Deer Unc George:

Mama and I went to a town cald Baltamor this wk, and a man on the train askt her for a drink with him. I said Mama doesnt need it, her suitcase is loaded with liker. Mama said it was a small bottle of perfume you guv her last week. Mama didnt like it I said that to the man.

Barbie

Baltimore

Dear George:

Baltimore is still lovely and people walk slowly in Charles Street. Aunt Hat is better now and will be at home shortly. I offered to take her back to Spice Hill but she feels it would be more restful in her own home, Guilford.

I had a dreadful experience on the train. A very handsome colonel with all sorts of ribbons on his uniform sat in the club car next to us while Barbie and I were waiting to go into the diner and he made friends with her—you know she is so friendly—and he offered me a cocktail. Well, Barbie spoke right up and said I had a bottle in my suitcase that a nice man gave me. It was your perfume of course, but that would sound phony to explain.

So I had to have dinner with him just to prove I am really a lady. I hope. He was very nice and took such an interest in Barbie.

Lucia

Dear Uncle George:
I need a paint set liek you sent Rog. He used his allup.

Barbie

Spice Hill, September 6

Dear George:
I am so sorry I couldn't meet you for our evening in New York. I really meant to.

I pictured the whole thing, the nice dinner in that little French place you know everybody at, and the good play, and the dancing afterward. Honestly, George, it would have been such fun, and I had a new dress, a pale smoke color—and the baby sitter all engaged, and I think reliable, although I am never sure any more. I had my hair done, too, in a new way, and a manicure—nobody, but nobody would ever guess I had done a big washing and cleaned house and got the three Indians cleaned and fed.

I am telling you all so you won't think I am just an ungrateful woman, indeed I am not.

I wired you I could make it and just as I was getting the car out, and finding a flat tire and coming back to get the taxi, I found that Roger was in the back yard, and it may be my fault but he was so high up in the tree and I screamed, and he just plummeted down like a meteor.

I knew he wasn't dead because he began to yell so loudly. But I did feel I had to get the doctor and be sure, and then he had so many bruises and cuts—and Barbie got upset and began dancing up and down screaming, "My brother's killed, goody goody!" That upset Pudding, who began to wail in his pen.

So then I had to cancel the taxi and wait for the doctor and quiet the baby and give Barbie my jewel box to play with, and I just couldn't manage.

I hope you and Ruth Bell had a glamorous and happy evening.

Lucia

Dear Unc George:

That was a swell time last Satdy and Mom says I oughto thank you for taking me to the zoo. I liked the zebra and seal. And snakes. I and Duff are collecting, we found quite a bunch. We got cartons for them. We got one dozen at leas. It is a secret. Dont tell. Plese bring me a cage when you come—and I hop you come Friday not Satdy, I got lots to have you do.

Roger

Dear Unkle George:

I used my crayns all up. I wisht I had more. I wisht I had a kitten too. Plese come early next time, I have some things to show you.

Barbie

Spice Hill, Tuesday

Dear George:

The children are bothering me to have you come earlier this week end, if you can get away from the office. You could spend Friday night here, as Aunt Hat won't be leaving until Sunday.

I got so upset this week, because I was supposed to visit school for PTA and Roger left me a note saying, "Please Ma no fancy clothes." (He spelled it right too.) I never wear fancy clothes and I just didn't know what I was doing wrong. Then he phoned from school at noon while he had his lunch and said in this perfectly wild voice, "Please Ma, no *fancy clothes*." I was so worried I almost called you at the office to see what you would think I ought to wear. My clothes, as you know, are so plain. Then Bebe Thomson dropped in for tea and I said I was due the next morning at this thing, and she just laughed and said, "Well, Lucia, no matter what you wore, you'd look *different* and not like the run-of-the-mill mothers."

George, do you think I dress suitably?

Lucia

Dear Uncle George:

There is a problem come up at my school which is the Father son banquet with stunts. The fathers do nutty things and all and the kids holler. It is kind of neat. I mean everybuddy is there and all but no mothers.

It is Fridy nite and you could wear that neat tie you had when you and Mom went off and left us all evening. Period.

Roger

Spice Hill, Sunday

Dear George:

I am so terribly sorry you missed that appointment with the Cleveland buyer on account of staying so long at that dinner with Roger and missing the last train and having to spend the night at the inn. I told Roger ahead of time you were a very busy and important man and had no time for these things and Roger said simply, "Nuts." Then he asked if you were rich and I told him something or other and he said, "It figures." What could he have meant?

Anyhow I gather you were the hit of the evening with that imitation of the Green Hornet in Times Square. And Roger had felt so—disgraced not to have a father.

I mean, I am so grateful. But I think you are spending too much time on my children, even rocking the baby when she has colic and singing Old Aunt Rhody. So I do hope you will take Ruth Bell to the Company dinner, she is such a lovely person and so beautiful and so poised and has no problems, if you follow me.

If you do come out Friday night, would you bring some French bread from La Patisserie?

Lucia

Dear Uncle George:

Why I am now writing is I liked the beech picnic a lot. It was neat and I thot you mite cum out for anuther this Friday nite. Mom says no, but I thot mabe you could cansel yur dates and do it if I ast you. Duffy Gordon wants to cum too if we go, so to see how you do the hot dogs on those sticks. His Father cant do it.

Roger

Spice Hill, Sept. 30

Dear George:

No, I can't make the dinner. I am a Den Mother and this is the night for the jamboree and when I merely suggested, Roger's eyes went just black and he said, why doesn't Uncle George come to our jamboree? You see, I feel I have to be responsible.

Lucia

Spice Hill, Oct. 2

Dear George:

I think it would be best if we did not see each other any more. I am sure the dinner was fine and Ruth Bell would make a fine hostess for the staff and of course she has no other ties, being a career woman, and the jamboree was fine too, except the boys rather wrecked the house, there being no man to keep them in order. But I do the best I can.

Lucia

Telegram to Mr. George Blakeslee from Mrs. Lucia Browning, October 5:

CANNOT MEET YOU. ROGER ILL. SORRY. LUCIA

Spice Hill, Oct. 10

Dear George:

I do hope it didn't upset your Chicago conference but I do thank you for coming out to the hospital. I just couldn't seem to cope. Now that it is all over and Roger only has a virus, I can only say I do thank you. I do.

Lucia

Dear Uncle George:

Know what I thot of? I thot too bad no more beech picnics and zooes for yours truly. I am very neat now and home tomorrow and can you come Friday as per usual so we can start bldg that jet plane? Barbie ast me to say can you cum too.

Roger

St. Mary's Hospital, Oct. 11

Dear George:

Mrs. Magnusson is doing fine with the baby. He has a little rash that worries me and I can't leave Roger just yet and I get absurdly anxious although I know Mrs. Magnusson has had five children and is so faithful and so sensible. I keep staring out of this hospital window, wondering about Pudding and Barbie. I think I can take Roger home tomorrow. I certainly hope so.

Lucia

Spice Hill, October 13

Dear George:

I never can thank you enough for coming right over and seeing about Pudding and Barbie. When you phoned that you had to fly to Chicago, I felt so lost, somehow, but when I got home with Roger and found a complete dinner all cooked and ready to reheat, plus the flowers, plus the latest magazines by my bedside, plus the new games for the children, I don't mind admitting I sat right down without even taking my hat off and bawled. Mrs. M. said you had been out just before you left for the plane and what she said about you would turn your ears lobster-colored.

With love,
Lucia

Dear Uncle George:

You wasnt around when I cum home and I felt you should of stood here when I came not go off to chicago like that. Mom says you earn a living and probly you do, I hope. Ha ha.

If you get back next week I could work on the jet plane, I am week but very O.K. and the hospitl was quite neat.

Roger

Spice Hill, Oct. 20

Dear George:

We are all in good shape at the moment and I am knitting you a sweater. Roger is back in school and we had Sadie Hawkins Day, which means the girls pin colored bows on the boys they like best and the boys pin back more bows. I made two for Roger and he said hesitantly maybe I better make a couple extra. He came home with 16 bows on his shirt. It looks as if we are raising a glamour boy!

Lucia

Dear Uncle George: I have a brain injury

Roger

Dear George:

I am so sorry you left the office and rushed out after getting Roger's note. It was very clever of you to realize, however, as you reached Stamford, that if he had a serious brain injury he couldn't have written to you. All that happened was that he got in an argument with Duffy as to whether you were his real father or not and Duffy bashed his head in with a croquet mallet. It was not serious at all and I am sorry about the whole thing.

I am increasingly anxious about the time you spend running in and out from the city to Spice Hill. I feel it is not a very good way for you to live. A person can't be always jumping about and taking that dreadfully late train back and then getting to the office at nine in the morning.

I planted the tulip bulbs you brought and the spring garden will be just heavenly. The children just loved the new game and have it all over the living room. You seem to always know just what they will like best.

Lucia

Dear Uncle George:

You better cum out, I am in a fix. I never ment to lok the lady in the tiket booth at the movies and hide the kees, a guy said you darent and I dared. This is Q T Mom can't be in on it. If you lost 5 dollars pay I will pay back when I can get a paper route when legal old enuf, now you better just cum and fix.

Roger

Spice Hill, Nov. 1

Dear George:

What a surprise when you came out in the middle of the week and picked Roger up at school! Why ever did you do it? But it was a godsend that you had the car to get Barbie in since I just couldn't start the old *thing* at all that day.

Barbie ate up all the cheese you brought.

Lucia

Deer Unkle Georg:

Roger maks me writ this and he mails it by himself. He says too much comming and gooing and you culd have the sew room for yours.

Barbie

Spice Hill, November 4

Dear George:

It just isn't any use. I got all dressed up again and wanted to give you a merry evening, as you deserve, when the baby sitter phoned that she had just come down with mumps. I just hated it. We could have had such a gay evening together. I hope it wasn't too late for you to get Ruth Bell, and I feel sure it wasn't and I hope you both had a lovely, lovely time, all spangled and shiny.

Lucia

Dear Uncle George:

I am sneeking this off. I think you better cum out. Mom is crying lots. I ast her if she has a toothache. She said no. I guess it was too bad she had to stay home last Satdy nite and miss going to the big city. I guess that wuld have been neat. She had her hare dun agin.

Roger

Dear Unk George:

Roger says I ast you to bring me a panda.

Barbie

Spice Hill, Nov. 7

Dear George:

I have told you how it is. I have the three children and it is such a crew! They just aren't your responsibility and there it is. You deserve—you deserve everything.

Lucia

Dear Uncle George:

I lost a tooth and I sav it in a dish for you to see, it is the last I lose. The others I lose at camp this summer. I am now grown.

Roger

Spice Hill, Nov. 10

Dearest George:

I feel as if I have stars at my fingertips. Somehow this last week end, when the children were all in such a state, and you came and managed everything. And even the baby stopped hiccoughing. I love you, I loved you the first minute I saw you leaning against the Nortons' trestle table and quirking your eyebrows in that easy and wonderful way. I love your steadiness and your intelligence. , But darling, my darling, I never would have given in and said I'd marry you except for one thing. When you said last Saturday night as we tucked the children in and cleaned up the kitchen and turned on the radio and you said so thoughtfully that we would have to plan a honeymoon some place where the children would have plenty of things to do, then I *knew*.

Your own Lucia

Spice Hill, Nov. 12

Darling:

A week from Wednesday is all right. But I hope you won't mind, George, I have wired Aunt Hat to come and take care of the children for two weeks. I just thought on our honeymoon—if it doesn't bother you too much, let's leave the children at home!

Your very own Lucia

Dear Uncle George:

This is to ast you for a favvor. Would you be on the Father son team for baseball next time? I culd help you practise. Duff's old man is a pretty good socker, but neat.

Mom says you are going on a short trip with us behind with old Aunt Hat but I guess that is O.K. as long as you get back in time to practise some.

Roger

Spice Hill, Nov. 14

Darling:

I do hope you realize you are taking on a whole family. Until tomorrow, it isn't too late.

But I know you have had a whole family for some time.

We all love you.

Lucia

Look Homeward, Dusty

✿✿✿✿✿✿✿✿✿✿✿✿ ✿

He walked a little stiffly because it was a damp day. His left hind leg bothered him. His muzzle had gone a little gray, as if it had been frosted. Several of his teeth were worn down, so it took him a long time to eat a dog biscuit. His eyelids drooped a trifle, although the dark eyes were still clear.

He was eight years old, a compact, deep-coated black cocker spaniel, with nobly shaped head, low sweeping ears, and the big bones from generations of fine breeding. He was listed as Champion Dusty Night of Old Rock Kennels.

His ribbons and cups and salad bowls and platters and pitchers made a nice display in the office, but some of them were getting tarnished and the color had ebbed from the purple in the rosettes. For they were old.

This morning he sat by the kennel gate, anxious, nose

quivering. For the station wagon was rolled out, the show cases were being piled up and the Master was hurrying around the yard. The old routine was beginning, and Dusty lifted his head and watched and waited.

Now was the time to put him up, give him a last brush and polish, wrap his own bath towel around him, tuck him in his case. An old traveler, he would sleep while the station wagon bucketed across the country.

Then the show. In anticipation he stood up, lifting his right front paw slightly the way he did when he was excited. The show was his life, had always been his life.

That long-gone day when he went into the puppy class, the Master had trimmed him, brushed him, posed him, combed the long feathers, carried him to the edge of the ring.

"I expect a lot of you," he said.

Dusty heard the urgency in his voice, and his tail answered. In the ring, the smell of the other dogs was heady, the lights were sharp, the noise of the spectators was loud. He stood quietly, looking with that open, candid gaze at the judge, he posed rock-still, head up, the lovely hind-quarters angled just so, though it was slightly uncomfortable to have one's paws so far back that way.

And when he moved down the ring, his gait was perfect, and the excitement of the whole thing swept over him so that he wagged his tail, and his nose was proud and eager.

"A born show dog," said the Master.

Leaving the show, wrapped in his towel, Dusty looked back. And suddenly he uttered a bark, rich with triumph. "Sure you did it," said the Master, rubbing his sleek head. "How'd you like to be a champ?"

He took his responsibilities seriously; he was a grave dog. He learned not to lower his head when he was moving down the ring, no matter what special scent might be there. He learned to stiffen a little when the judge pressed down on his hind quarters, emphasizing his solid strength. And he always came into the ring with a swift, purposeful gait, his tail whipping, eyes shining.

This was his life, the way of it, and it had always been so.

And then, one day, the Master went off and left him in the run. Half a dozen other dogs got in the station wagon and drove away barking like fools. And Dusty stayed home with a couple of twelve-week-old bitches that had to be snapped at for ear-swinging.

He watched all day at the gate. Maybe the Master had forgotten him and would come swinging up the drive and take him out.

In the end, when it was dark, he gave up and lay down with his muzzle on his paws, trying still to figure what he had done that was wrong, so he had to be punished so dreadfully.

After that day, he was never taken along on the show trips. Always he knew when the time came, and pranced to the gate, and bounded up against it. He used to find one of the puppy's red balls and bring it too as a special offering. Jumping against the gate, ball in mouth, tail pleading, eyes anxious, he waited until the sound of the motor died away in the distance. Once some people came and stood outside the run and looked at him.

"Yes, that's the one," said the Master. "Of course he's too old to show now, but he's a good sire. Best dog I ever had."

His coat grew rough, nobody trimmed him any more. He had a good clean bed, plenty of fresh cool water and his own bowl of dogfood at feeding time. For the rest, he dozed in the sun or ran briefly up and down the run. He gave up the ball-carrying after a time; it did no good.

He noticed that particular day that there was even more activity than usual around the place. A moving van backed up and loaded boxes and furniture on it. Some people came and took away a brace of puppies. The Master was hurrying all over the yard.

A faint hope stirred him when five dogs were put in cases and the last puppies were led away. Surely he would not be the only one left behind! This time he would go, this time there would be a ring and the judge and the crowd and the excitement. He ran up and down the fence line.

He was panting, limping a little, his eyes bright with hope. Yes, this time it was true. The Master came and picked him up.

"This one goes East," he said to a man with him, "I couldn't sell him somehow. He and I—we went through the big time together when we were young." He rubbed Dusty's ears. Dusty quivered with love and joy.

"Champion, ain't he?" asked the other.

"Yeah. I'm shipping him back to Mrs. Windsor. She owned his sire and bred the litter Dusty was in. I got the pup when he was eight weeks old."

"How old is he now?"

"Going on nine. Try to get him to the airport to catch the noon plane, will you? Quicker trip. Kind of hate to see him start flying at his age. But Mrs. Windsor will give him a good home, she was crazy over the sire and crazy over that litter."

He put Dusty in the traveling case. Dusty was wagging his tail. "No, son, we've seen our last show. This is the end of the line." And he walked away very fast.

Dusty eased down in the case, but kept his nose awake for the familiar scent of the show, dogs, disinfectant, perfume, smoke. But he was put in a strange dim place and set down. Noises came to him, not any known sounds, the smell was strange, his water dish slopped a little. Suddenly he felt dizzy. The air was odd. It was dark. He didn't eat at all, his stomach was too full of ache. Not hunger ache, but sorrow ache.

It was endless, and then it ended and he was carried out into an open field. But no flags waving, no barking, no kennelmen running around. Just an empty field. A man took him out on his leash and he politely found a small uninspired bush, and felt better.

But there was no sign of the Master, he was alone in an alien world, and the sickness was in his bones.

A woman came running across the field. "There he is!" she cried, "there's Dusty! I'd know him anywhere! Come on, boy!"

He couldn't understand, but he greeted her nicely, trotted off with her.

There was a car waiting, not his station wagon. When he was told to, he got in, and sat in dignified stiffness on the floor.

Another trip, this traveling was a long thing. He could have howled his heart out, but that wasn't the way a gentleman did. The next thing he knew, he was taken into a house, the leash unsnapped and he was free.

This was the strangest place of all. There were five or six cockers, untrimmed, running around; there were a couple of cats. The cockers rushed at him, and sniffed him thoroughly, and made whuffling noises. The cats hissed and got on the table.

Dusty found a corner and sat in it, paws together, eyes wary. There was a sickness in his bones. After a while they all let him alone, and went racketing around the house. The woman brought him a bowl. It had fresh chopped beef in it, his special treat after a show.

But he turned his head away. He didn't want to eat. The woman picked him up in her arms and sat down with him in a big chair. He looked at her with great sad eyes.

"Darling, don't be too homesick," she said; "it will be better after a while." And she kissed him right on the top of his head.

She was a nice person. A little of the stiffness went out of his tired legs. The floor stopped swaying so much. When she put him down, he felt he might as well follow her. So he stuck to her heels all day, upstairs, downstairs, in and out.

Nobody was getting any of the dogs ready for a show. There weren't any cases around, no trimming table, and he couldn't see a single trophy on any wall or on any shelf.

He had been in a house now and then, when the Master brought him in to show him to somebody. He got up on a trimming table, then posed, then went back to the run. But this was different. All the dogs ran around freely, picking various things out of a big basket by the fireplace, and playing games with them. He watched, and wondered; he had never seen anything like it in his whole life.

"You feeling hungry now?" asked the woman after a while.

She put down a bowl, and just to please her, he ate the whole meal, and polished the dish so it wouldn't have to be cleaned. Then he felt well enough to move slowly to the water bowl and take a long drink, establishing his right to do so. Pretty good water, not as good as in the kennel, but all right.

She let him out and he cruised carefully around the yard, bigger than any exercise ring in the world, and really rather fine. When she opened the door he came right back in, and he saw a couple of the dogs sitting up on the sofa. This was a strange place.

He thought about that for awhile and then ventured to get up too, and it was fine and soft to lie on. He was fearfully tired now. Confused, anxious, lost, his heart beat slowly, his legs was stiff.

In the night, he got to feeling so bad he couldn't stand it. Where was his Master? Here it was night, he was not in his kennel, not at a show. It was too much.

Paw by paw, he crept out of the room, found the scent of the woman and followed it. He knew how to climb stairs, he had done that at indoor shows in the past. He heard her breathing upstairs in the front room. Dusty went up to the door and scratched at it and it opened and he moved across the soft thick rug. He put tentative paws on the edge of the bed, leaned his muzzle wistfully on the bedcover.

"Not feeling so good?" she said. "Come on up with me, then."

Dusty got on the bed, and her hand was warm and

comfortable on his left ear, and he gave a sigh big enough to burst his lungs and stretched out beside her.

It was too soft, really, and he wouldn't sleep there again. But it was very nice to know he could, if he wanted to.

They were all put out in a run the next day and the woman drove off. She did not take anybody else to a show; he watched and not a single one went. He sat close to the gate, blinking a little in the bright sunlight.

Well, here he was again, in a kennel, with nothing to occupy him except a feeling of loss. Now the only difference was that there was grass under paw instead of gravel, and the air smelled sharper.

She had gone away, where? A fly bumbled around and he snapped it up, but without interest. The others played bones and dug holes and jumped around. They left him all by himself. His left hind leg began to ache and he coughed a little. His head drooped.

Suddenly he heard the sound of her car and she came back walking lightly over the grass. Without any hope, he watched her come. She would pick out a couple of the others and there would be the snap of the leash and they would go away. He would get a bowl of food and a drink of water.

"Well, come on in, everybody," said the woman, and opened the gate. Dusty didn't move for an instant. "Come on, darling," she said, laughing.

He rushed to the gate, fearful, eager. But it was not closed on his muzzle! They all went with the woman into the house, unleashed.

The others were bounding against the woman, dashing off to bring favorite bones from hiding places obvious to anybody's nose. Two leaped to that soft couch. The cats appeared, stretching and yawning delicately. They hissed mildly as he passed, but more as a gesture than anything else.

The house was full of confusion and noise and the good smell of chopped beef drifting from a package on the table. The woman was dishing out bowls of it. She looked at his wistful eyes. "This is your own bowl," she said, "the blue one. For always."

He could never have imagined a life like this, never.

But now, suddenly, he knew it was all his. He began to run in crazy circles, in and out of the room, around and about. There was that box of treasures—clean old bones, leather shoes, knotted woolen socks! He whirled past it, checked his mad flight, nose-dived and came up with a red ball.

Head lifted proudly, tail going wildly, Champion Dusty Night of Old Rock, grave veteran of the show ring, bounced across the room carrying the ball. She was in the other room by the stove and he ran so fast he shot right past her, and had to turn to get back to her. He held up the ball, panting with excitement.

Smiling, she bent down and took it, and tossed it. He chased it, skating across a small rug, and jumping on it with fierce delight when he caught it.

Almost like a puppy!

Money of
Her Own

❉❉❉❉❉❉❉❉❉❉❉   ❉

It was missionary season. In those days, they came once a year and gave talks in the Methodist, Presbyterian, Congregational churches to gather funds for the Lord's work. Sometimes they were just back from Rangoon or some other place in Burma, sometimes from Japan or China. Once a Reverend Mr. MacLean came from Ceylon. Sometimes, of course, they only came from Chicago from the mission office, without glamour, wreathed in no glory.

Missionary season was always a time of unrest at the Prentice house. Mother loved missionaries and would have given every cent we had to each and every one. But Father felt differently.

"You keep away from them," he warned; "all they want is money. Take every red cent if they could."

"But, Richard," said Mother, "we have to do our

duty by the heathen! Think of those benighted souls with nobody but missionaries. . . ."

"Nonsense," said Father, "they have their own governments. Why don't we stay home and mind our own business?"

Mother's color was high; she had a delicate skin and flushed easily, and looked wonderfully young and pretty when she did. "Richard Prentice, don't you care whether they are saved or not?"

"Pass the potatoes," said Father, with dignity. "I tell you, Laura, if I had to have my soul saved by that last specimen you dragged home for supper, I'd rather not *be* saved."

Mother set her lips. They were too absorbed to notice I was drinking the vinegar left in the bottom of my salad plate. How good it was, salted and peppered and still flavored faintly with cucumber. Father said it would eat out the lining of my stomach, and Mother said it just wasn't the thing to do. So I always had trouble about it.

"And I don't want you throwing away my money," said Father firmly. "I have contributed generously to the fund for repairing the pews and fixing up the organ, and that's enough."

"Father, may I have a quarter?" I asked.

He fished out his snap purse and gave me a quarter. His bright blue eyes twinkled. "Make it go as far as possible," he said.

I always knew when I could get a little petty cash outside of my twenty-five cents a week. This gave Father a chance to show how really generous he was, that it was purely the principle of the missionary business he was against, that for his loved child, he would spare no quarters; but asking for money for the heathen was foolish.

"Is there any more of the strawberry shortcake?" he asked.

Mother cut a thick wedge. The whipped cream melted into the rich red juices, the shortcake was feather-light.

All week, the missionary struggle went on. Mother would slip up to church and listen breathlessly to the lectures, and I went too. In the dim light of the church parlor the pale thin spinster would talk a long, long time, and the minister would speak too, and the portable blackboard would be covered with figures.

Mother and I would hurry home in the early dusk, arriving just before Father came home for supper.

"I wish they'd tell more about what it's like over there," I said.

"Yes," said Mother. "I wish so too. I would like to know what it's like inside a pagoda."

Mother got supper in a hurry, but Mother was the best cook in town and Father never suffered during the days she went to church. Country-fried potatoes, crisping at the edges, rosy slices of ham baked in mustard sauce, the first picking of asparagus from the garden, and rhubarb pie with a crust light enough to look through, several cups of coffee, and Father would have had enough until the bedtime snack.

This particular spring, Mother had managed to save a little here and there, and this was the way a woman did in those days. Father paid the bills on the first of the month and there were charge accounts for everything. If Mother needed anything, she could get it and charge it and then explain about it when the bill came. She had to ask for cash for the streetcar and for her Wednesday club dues. I was better off than she was, for I had a quarter of my own every week. But there was a chain store on Main Street where you paid cash for everything and got things for less. Father found out and gave Mother some money to be used for specials at the chain store.

And Mother was a genius at managing. She could buy the cheapest cuts of meat and turn out roasts better than rolled rib. A turnip was a challenge to her, and what she did with plain winter carrots was definitely her own business. So Father ate on, unmindful of the small roll of dollar bills in her purse.

"I am going to have something for the missionary fund," Mother said to me. "I feel I must. But it won't be enough for my share."

I could see it worried her, for she was as sunny and open by nature as a daisy field. But this missionary business went deep with her. All her longing to do good, and all her yearning just to have some contact with those faraway people and places—just to feel that she somehow had something to do with some little grass-roofed hut at the jungle's edge. . . .

Everything was fine. Mother baked an angel food for the silver tea and made little filled cookies and the ladies of the society all said nobody could cook like mother. No one could. I passed the cake basket so I could have three pieces with no attention drawn to myself.

And Mother had just put another dollar bill in her purse after buying a flank steak on the way home, instead of the tenderloin Father had suggested. Flank steak didn't cost anything in those days. Braised with vegetables, it was perfect.

After supper, Father went to a lodge meeting and I

went upstairs, ostensibly to do my grammar but really to read *Spinner in the Sun.* I heard the doorbell ring and peered down the stairwell, and saw our Polish neighbor was there. The Plinkos lived at the bottom of the hill, and the father worked in the mill. Since he was a drinking man, Father thought little of him and assumed the children must take after him.

Mrs. Plinko was crying and had a black shawl over her head. Mother let her in and they went into father's study and mother closed the door. I crept down and listened as hard as I could, but the door was good and solid. When Mother suddenly opened the door, I was knocked off my feet. Mother looked pale and determined.

"Get me my pocketbook," she said.

She didn't even bother about my eavesdropping. I got her pocketbook.

"Go upstairs and do your homework," she said.

I went slowly enough to look back on every step and I saw mother take out the little worn morocco purse and open it. I saw her take the missionary money in her hand and go back to the study and close the door behind her.

I sank right down on the stairs. Mamma was giving away all the money she'd saved for the heathens! It couldn't be, and yet it was! I sat there hugging my knees until the door opened a last time and Mrs. Plinko was ushered out, incoherent with thanks and still sniffling.

"Mamma! Mamma!" I cried, running down. "You gave her the heathens' money!"

Mother said, "She's in trouble, she needed it."

She went to the kitchen and put the kettle on for coffee, a sure sign that she was agitated beyond help.

"Mamma, what was it?"

"No need to discuss it," said Mother. "I only want you to remember that wine is a mocker, strong drink is raging."

"Oh," I said. "Did they cut off the gas and the water, too, this time?"

"Never mind," said Mamma. "And I will say that I think it is a mistake for the sins of the fathers to be visited on the children. Get out the peanut butter if you want a sandwich."

"You aren't going to tell Father, are you?"

Mother pushed her brown hair back. "There is no need to worry him."

The sign of her conflict was still on her set mouth. What a dreadful choice, between the heathen and the neighbors, for that hard-saved money.

And there was no time to go through all the pinching and planning and saving again. The missionary fund would be collected, sealed, signed and delivered Sunday morning. But there wouldn't be any pale brown envelope signed R. D. Prentice.

"Oh, Mamma," I said, "if only you could get the money! If only father would. . . ."

Mother drank her coffee, hot and black. "There must be a way," she said; "there must be a way."

Father came home then, and said the refreshments at the lodge weren't any good, so he'd like something fit to eat.

Mother scrambled eggs with onion and cheese the way he liked them, and poured more coffee and cut a fresh loaf of her good bread.

"This is more like," said Father happily.

"Richard," said Mother, "I want to ask you to change your mind about the missionary fund."

Father buttered his bread. "Change my mind? Why should I, when I know I'm right?"

"But I don't think you are right," persisted Mother, getting pink.

"I," said Father, "am not a sentimental woman."

"Even a man," said Mother, "should have concern for his fellow creatures."

"That's right," said Father, getting red too, "accuse me of being hardhearted just because I won't send my money gallylogging." He dished up the rest of the eggs. "I have a family to support," he said nobly, "and if you had your way, I suppose we'd go bankrupt while your heathens rolled in riches."

"The money you might contribute to the missionary fund," said Mother, "would certainly not keep us from bankruptcy. Of that I am sure."

"Father, may I have a quarter?" I asked.

Father gave me a look, and then handed out a quarter. Well, I could give Mamma fifty cents now for her fund. But what was fifty cents? Even if they argued all night, I couldn't get more than one more quarter out of it. "Go on to bed now," he said, "or you'll never get up in the morning."

I could hear them as I braided my long pigtails. Father got madder and madder; they were going all over the heathen again, and the missionaries and the church. And when they came upstairs, Father was shouting, "Not one cent of my money, and that's final."

He slammed around getting ready for bed, and Mother went to the sewing room and threaded the machine. I could hear the foot pedal going. When she was really angry, she would sew feverishly far into the night. Mother wouldn't shout back at Father, but she had plenty of spirit and she wouldn't meekly settle down after an argument. She would sew, and that, I thought, made Father simply wild.

"Laura, aren't you coming to bed?"

"I have a little stitching to do."

"Laura, it's late. You better come to bed."

"After a while."

"You'll never get up in the morning if you don't get to bed at night."

"I don't feel sleepy."

"Don't blame me if you have a sick headache tomorrow."

"I won't," said Mother sweetly. "I thought I'd mend some of my old underwear and give it to the missionary barrel."

Father gave a groan and said no more.

After a little, I got up and went into the sewing room. Mother was running the treadle rapidly, her hair was loosened under the silk hair net, and her eyes looked very dark and bright.

"You ought to be asleep," she said.

"Mamma, why is Father so mean?"

"He isn't mean," she answered, stopping the machine. "He is just convinced about things. He sees things in a— personal way. He can't believe in things outside the state much; that's the way a man is, I expect."

"Well," I said, "if I ever get married, my husband has got to give me five dollars a week, even if I want to throw it in the garbage."

"Oh, dear," said Mother. "Who ever heard of such a thing?" Then she turned and gave me a long, thoughtful look. Her face was pale and shadowy above the lace frill of her nightgown.

"Money of my own," she said slowly, "that I had a right to."

She went into such deep thought that I moved away and got back to bed. When she got one of her thinking spells, she never noticed anybody else until she was all through thinking.

The next morning there were waffles for breakfast with crumbled maple sugar and melted butter, and tiny country-sausage balls on the side. Father came downstairs at peace with the world after a good sleep and with the smell of waffles in his nose. Mother was deftly lifting a golden-brown waffle to a hot willowware plate. She wore her blue dress with the white collar and looked cool and serene.

Father kissed her. "Smells good," he said, "hope you made plenty." We all sat down, and Mother served the sausage and passed the cream.

"I've about made up my mind to give you a new stove," said Father, helping himself to brown curls of sugar. "I was talking to Will Bradley yesterday. Of course they are expensive, but they don't leak gas and there's a thing keeps 'em from smoking everything up. How does that idea strike you?"

"I'd rather have the money," said Mother.

"Money? What for? What money?"

Mother said calmly, "I've decided it would be very nice to have a little money of my own."

Father stared at her, thunderstruck. If she had threatened to elope with the garbage collector, he wouldn't have been any more astounded.

Then he got red. "I suppose I don't provide well enough for you," he said stiffly. "I suppose you wish you had married John Pettibone."

"Providing has nothing to do with it," said Mother. "I just want a little money to do with. So I think I'll earn some."

"Earn—earn money?" Father whispered hoarsely.

"That's what I thought," nodded Mother.

Then Father laughed, suddenly relieved. "What a notion! What an idea! You earn money? What fancies women get, the best of 'em. Just how did you think you would earn money?"

Mother looked at him steadily, a strange little smile curving her mouth. "I am going to earn it," she said, "by cooking."

"Cooking!"

"People will buy whatever I make," she said. "My things always go first at all the sales."

Father tried to speak, but couldn't.

"I can take orders," Mother said complacently. "It would be quite simple, really. I just never thought of it before."

Father rose, tall with dignity. "Laura Prentice," he said, "I cannot conceive of your being anything other than out of your wits to suggest such a thing. My wife, my own wife, out earning money! What do you think that would look like? Would you drag our name in disgrace? And our daughter's name?"

"Don't be dramatic," said Mother. "Everybody will understand."

"Laura," said Father, "when I am dead and in my grave, you may think of this hour when you shortened my life. But while I am still here, I ask you not to pursue this fantasy further." And leaving a whole waffle untouched, Father made a grand exit.

Mother said calmly, "You can finish his up if you like; he had gobs of butter on it."

"Mamma, you didn't mean it?"

"Never you mind. You go on to school. And you missed a chance for one of those quarters just now."

I could hardly wait to get home from school. But at noon, after I braked my bicycle and dashed in, my lunch was on the kitchen table with a note from Mother, saying she was out.

After school, there was an extra session of the chorus for those who couldn't keep on the key very well. So I didn't get home until nearly suppertime and I flew in. I dropped my books and dashed to the kitchen.

Mother had just come in. I knew because she had her overall apron on, and I could see her brown satin skirt swishing under the apron hem. She had on her best high-buttoned shoes too. Bacon was crisping in the iron spider, and Mother was slicing onions in the black kettle. Liver and bacon, I deduced. We had been eating liver a lot, it was so cheap.

"You can set the table," said Mother. "I haven't gotten to it yet. Father'll be in any minute."

She looked as quiet and calm as the lake in June, but she was calm just the way she was when she took my temperature and didn't know what I might be coming down with this time.

I heard Father then, pounding up the back steps, and

I hurried to the dining room with a load of plates. The sun was just setting and a clear pale glow came through the white curtains. The spring twilight lay under the trees like still water. It was so peaceful, and yet inside the house there was dynamite.

"What's this I hear? What's this about? What in the name of the Great Dipper has got into you?" This was Father just getting into his stride.

Mamma's voice was so cool, so light. "Richard dear, remember we do have neighbors, and they hear very well."

I went to the dining-room door and pushed it ajar. Mother was dipping slices of liver in flour, salt, and pepper.

"Laura Prentice!" Father was shouting. "I want to know what you've been doing!"

Mother faced him. "Why? What's the matter, Richard?"

"It's all over town!" shouted Father, almost beside himself. "All over town!"

"Oh," said Mother, "you mean about the tearoom?"

"Tearoom!" His voice was just a croak.

"Well," said Mother, "you know Libby Jones has been trying to get a partner so she can turn her house into one. Since Ben died, she's been thinking of it. But she needed someone who could really cook." Mother dropped the liver in the pan. "And you know you said I was the best cook in town yourself, Richard."

Father was practically royal purple and his mouth was tightened until I couldn't tell he had one, except there were words coming out. "You have any idea I'll permit you to run a restaurant. . . ."

"Tearoom," said Mother.

"My wife running a dirty filthy restaurant. . . ."

"A clean tearoom," said Mother.

Father filled the whole room. He was a masterful man at his quietest, now he was a complete army. "Of course it's nothing to you how I feel," he said, "going around behind my back getting ready to work in a restaurant. . . ."

"Tearoom," said Mother.

"Tearoom be confounded," roared Father.

I was trembling so the doorknob rattled in my hand. Nothing so dreadful had ever happened in the family. Mother had never really openly crossed Father before. She got around him, but now she was openly defying him, and Father knew it.

"Laura," he said heavily, "you can either give up this notion or give up me. You can take your choice!"

And suddenly a whole rocket burst of stars seemed to go off in my head. I pushed open the door and rushed in. "Mamma, you ought to leave him!" I cried wildly.

Father looked as if a rattlesnake had reared its head under the gas stove. But it was only that I sounded exactly like him. "I'll divorce you both!" he shouted. "Both of you!" And then he flung himself out the door and vanished.

"Mamma, aren't you going after him?" I cried.

"No," said Mother.

Then we were both crying, and Mother got her smelling salts in the little dark green bottle with the silver top and we smelled and sneezed. Mother was so strange I hardly knew her. So collected and calm and so dreadfully white. And yet she moved around putting the liver in the warming oven and setting the onions back farther.

And then the door banged and Father was back. "Supper's ready," said Mother.

Father stood by the table looking hard at her. And then he said, "Laura, if I give you fifty dollars for your missionaries will you stop this nonsense?"

Mother looked at him and the color began to come back into her cheeks. There was a long moment of silence before she spoke.

"Why, Richard," she said softly, "that's very generous of you."

"Will you?" he asked.

"I don't really want to go against you in anything," said Mother, "and of course if you really wish. . . ."

Father gave a heavy sigh. He reached for his wallet and pulled out some crisp new bills and laid them on the table.

"There," he said, "there you are, Laura. I didn't know you had your whole heart set on those—those confounded dispensers of long underwear."

And then they forgot me completely, for Mother went right into his arms and he kissed her, not just a good-morning peck but quite, quite differently. So much so that I felt a sudden dreadful pang of loneliness and I hated them both for leaving me alone.

Then Father saw me and swung me up in his arms as if I didn't weigh anything, and kissed me too. Mother's hair net was entirely demolished and her soft brown hair flying around her face.

"Oh, Richard," she said, "all the souls you help to save will bless your name!"

"They can mind their own business," said Father. "When I need my name blessed, I'll take it up with God myself." Then he looked at the stove. "Supper about ready?" Emotion always made him very hungry.

"Just a minute," said Mother. She tucked the money into the teapot on the shelf.

"And I hope you're satisfied," said Father.

We had supper just as if it were any day. Father was very fond of liver and bacon and onions. He ate three helpings, and two of the Boston cream pie. His only comment was, "Seems to me we haven't had a tenderloin for some time."

"We can have one tomorrow," said Mother.

She wouldn't be pinching for this missionary fund any longer, I thought. Life would be peaceful again—as peaceful, that is, as our life ever was.

Father was gentle as a dove. He gave me a quarter voluntarily when I went up to do my homework and offered to wash the dishes. Mother let him, although I knew she dreaded it. When Father washed the dishes he scrubbed everything so violently with scouring powder that it was never the same again, and he splashed so much that Mother always had to clean the floor afterward. He even scrubbed the wedding silver with scouring powder, but Mother said not a word.

I could hear the sound of Father's battle in the kitchen, and Mother singing to herself as she put away the dishes, "From Greenland's icy mount-tains—to India's coral strand. . . ."

I went to my window and looked out at the dark sky drifted with stars. Would those heathen ever know what the Prentice family had suffered for them? No, they never would. How many souls would Father's blood money save? Fifty dollars was a fortune! Would Father give fifty dollars next year when the missionaries were back? This I doubted.

Would God credit this money to Father or only to Mother? God would know the reason for Father's doing it. It was just to keep Mother from working for money in a restaurant.

I was still standing there when Mother came upstairs and said, "You better go to bed, dear." The starlight fell on her face, and it was beautiful.

Father was banging away downstairs with his going-to-bed flurry.

Mother came over and stood beside me and looked out. "What a big, wonderful world," she said softly, "and how thankful we should be to be in it."

"Mamma, is everything all right?" I asked.

"Everything is fine," said Mother, and she put her arm around me. A star fell, blazing down the deep sky.

"Father wouldn't really divorce us, would he?"

"No," said Mother. "Father is a wonderful man." She pushed back her hair and bent to kiss me good night. "Still," she said, half to herself, "it would really be great fun to run a tearoom!"

Letter to
the Dean

State University
Monongahela
Office of the Dean of Women

Mrs. Kenneth March
Riverside
New York

My dear Mrs. March:

Your daughter's credentials are now complete and we hope that she will be with us at State University next year.

The office of the Dean of Women exists for the purpose of serving the women students; all that concerns the life of the campus is our responsibility. Our function is to offer assistance and advice in the difficult process of adjusting to a new environment which the new student faces.

Therefore we are asking your co-operation in order that we may assist your daughter in making a satisfactory and happy beginning. We should like you to write us frankly and freely and objectively about your daughter, telling us fully about her health, ambitions, temperament, and tastes. While the letter will of course be strictly confidential, it will be of great help to us in supervising your daughter's welfare.

Cordially yours,
Elizabeth Winthrop
Dean of Women

Miss Elizabeth Winthrop
Dean of Women
State University
Monongahela

My dear Miss Winthrop:

I have your letter asking me to write you about my daughter, frankly, freely and objectively.

My daughter Mary is sixteen. Her birthday is December. [*I didn't want to have a baby. I wasn't the kind of girl you read about who has one eye on the wedding ring and the other on a Kiddie Koop. I liked to stop on the street and admire fat little bundles done up in pink or blue and smelling of milk and talcum and damp diapers. But then I wanted to walk on, swinging my skates over my shoulder, or swishing off clover heads with my tennis* racket. I wanted to drive fast in the roadster with the top down, and dance late, and canoe down the big river at night under a tender moon. Something in me was always trying to escape—to be more free—to be just my own self, alone. Separate.

I was frightened. Something dark and formless reached around me and smothered me. I could never get away again. My throat was full of fear. I walked the floor and cried and bit my lips until blood and rouge were mixed. Yes, I beat my hands together and cried. And then of course I felt sick and dizzy from crying, and I was sure that was because I was going to have a baby.

But I didn't dare tell anybody how it was with me. Maybe it wasn't so bad to be a coward if nobody found it out. So I told Kenneth casually, and he said it was just marvelous and weren't we going to be happy. How would I like to celebrate with Chop Suey at the Chinese Pavilion? I've never been able to eat Chop Suey since. And afterward Kenneth bought me some long-stemmed roses, and I thought flowers for the funeral, the death of my youth.

We were very gay and smart about it, and then Kenneth sneaked away to his desk, and I could see him getting out his insurance policies and making figures on yellow scratch paper, and I knew he was afraid too. Babies cost money. And he was just getting started, and we just about got by on his salary at the bank.

Nine months is a long time. Getting up in the night to chew dry soda crackers or drink hot milk trying not to feel so ill. Being clumsy and heavy and wearing sloppy clothes. Aching feet and cold hands. A knife nicking away in your back. Fatigue like a heel pressed in your *temples. Oh yes, a fine thing for a girl who wasn't ready, who still wanted to run—to fly.*

Snow came early that year. It was the long winter. Snow was falling on the 23rd of December. It was dusk and I had been in the house all day. My lungs were tight with heated furnace air. So I bundled up and crept slowly around the block, feeling snow on my dry mouth, bracing my body against the throbbing, kicking of that other life. Lights were on, Christmas trees shone through the windows, and at the Gregorys' they were dancing. I could see Kathleen Gregory, light and slim and smooth, doing an intricate step with Phil; she wasn't as good as I had been, but of course the Kenneth Marches regretted. Kenneth was doing some extra work at the bank, worrying about the hospital expenses.

I heard the music and laughter and I looked hungrily at the lights, and wondered if another Christmas would find me fixing a tree or whether Kenneth would be carrying a wreath to the cemetery. It would be funny if I should die and Kenneth would have to start all over again. Just as I had learned to make cocoanut-cream pie, too.

The snow fell deep and heavy, but my cheeks were hot. Thoughts pounded in my head, almost too fast to sort out, the way they do sometimes. It must be strange to be dead and not know whether it is snowing or daffodils are out. That would be a terrible thing, not to know what season it was. I wished I had a mother, who would talk to me, and rock me in warm strong arms and stand between me and my fear. If I died, would Kenneth marry the Williams girl? She would be pretty glad if I died, she was wild about Ken, I knew it.

*Then my baby would be brought up by a stepmother.
I stopped and wiped snow crystals from my lashes. My
teeth were chattering. That minute I thought about it
as my baby, when I thought about a stepmother. No,
please God, please, please, I said, please don't have another woman take care of my baby. It's not fair, it's not
fair to do that.*

*Suppose, I thought then, that the baby isn't all right.
There was George Macintyre, who lived on Peach Street.
When I was a little girl he was there, sitting on the front
porch in an old rocking chair. All day long he sat and
rocked, and grinned, and he rocked so hard the chair
almost stood on end. They said he was forty years old,
and he wore the clothes of a fourteen-year-old boy.
Sometimes his mother came out and stopped the rocking
chair, and then he would cry like a baby until she went
away and let him rock again. Suppose my child was like
that? Forgetting that I was dead and under the ground
with Ken laying wreaths on my grave, I went through
a lifetime of waiting on a child who rocked all day long
and grinned and had to be fed with a spoon. No, please
God, no, no please, I begged.*

*I was crying to myself, so I missed the snow-deep curb,
and I fell down and as I fell a sword sliced right through
me. I couldn't get up for a minute, and then I stumbled
somehow to the door of the house and Kenneth was just
going in. "What in the world are you out in this blizzard
for?" he said sharply; and I said, "Call the Doctor, Kenneth, tell him to hurry."*

*But it was a whole day later when the Doctor said,
"You've got a fine beautiful baby girl, a Christmas present." I came out of the tangled jungle of pain and death*

and looked vaguely at what they held up for me to see. It was wrinkled and small and the color of a cinnamon drop and a small sound came from it. "You mean that's mine?" I whispered. "I think she looks like you," said the nurse. "Look at the beautiful shape of her head, and see all that dark hair?"

Kenneth was standing there and his face looked odd. He was crying. I said, "What in the world has upset you?" "I'm all right," he said gruffly, and turned his back. After awhile he came over and looked down. "I always wanted it to be a girl," he said shyly.

The nurse took her away and Kenneth and the Doctor went out. I could see that outside it was still snowing. All that time it had been snowing. And I was still alive and I had a baby in the nursery. A whole, perfect baby. My child, my daughter Mary.]

My daughter's health is excellent.

[It was funny when I rejected the idea of a baby, that I would hardly let her out of my sight after we were home again. Kenneth and I agreed that we wouldn't spoil her, no matter what. We had a book to raise her by, and when she cried Kenneth got out the book and read aloud to me what the book said. Then we would decide that she was simply crying to be picked up. "Just ignore her," Ken would say. "She's sick of lying there," I would say. So finally I would pick her up and just rock her a little bit, not enough to spoil her for good.

At night I always got to thinking perhaps she had too

much cover on. "Ken, do you think she has enough blankets?" "Now don't begin that again. We got to get some rest. She's all right." *I would hold out my hand, feeling the air. And listen to hear her breathe. I always argued half and hour and then got up and went in to put on a blanket and feel of her little face.*

But it was no good because then I'd get afraid she was too hot and if she got overheated she might catch cold; it might go into one of those respiratory diseases it told about in the book. By then it was usually around one, and I'd get up again and go in and take off a blanket. And feel her little curled fist.

"My God," *Ken said,* "you'll kill her covering and uncovering her all night the way you do."

But in some ways it was only a minute before she was trotting off to kindergarten in her blue bunny suit, with white overshoes on her little feet and her face framed in fur. She had grave dark eyes and coppery ringlets and a funny little nubbin of a nose and a firm mouth.

By the time she was in third grade she was asking for a baby brother or sister from Santa Claus, but by that time it was clear there couldn't be another baby. Santa Claus was nice about bringing rabbits and guinea pigs and kittens, though.

Kenneth insisted that I go with him on that business trip to Florida to inspect the bank investment. We had a maid by then, and we got a practical nurse and Mary was eight. We were only going to be away three weeks, he said, and he didn't think a vacation would do me any harm. We could dance and swim and have a time, he said.

Kenneth caught a blue marlin and I got sand fleas and we ate and drank a lot and swam. We could racket

*around day and night, just the way I always used to like.
I had a trunkful of new smooth clothes and a new haircut
and we learned to hum the new tunes off key. Ken said,
"You look like twenty." He said, "Isn't this swell? I'm
taking the rooms for another week." I walked up and
down the sun-bright streets near the sea looking at the
children. Once I saw a little girl in a blue dress with that
coppery shade of hair and I went quickly into the nearest
bar and had a drink. Then I bought a baby alligator, a
revolting thing, to send back to Mary. Every time I felt
bad I bought her something. I had three suitcases full of
what I bought.*

*When the phone call came, it was like something hap-
pening that I knew about. People must feel that way who
live at the edge of a volcano, when the flames finally do
erupt. Or when a building collapses. You see the first
swaying and the fault line of the concrete and then the
whole thing crashes, and you were waiting for it. The
nurse said, "We don't want to alarm you, Mrs. March,
but the doctor feels you better come home. It may be
pneumonia."*

*Ken was out on an all-day fishing trip. I didn't wait.
I caught the plane and then the train. I sat in the local
day coach and counted telephone poles. When I couldn't
focus on them any longer I counted cows and horses.
There was an Italian woman in the next seat with three
dirty little children. She fed them bananas and oranges
and chocolate; the smell of orange peel was strong. She
had three, all healthy, probably raised on a diet of spaghetti and garlic and red wine.*

*Please God she's all I have. Please God Please—please
listen to me. . . .*

When I got to the house I couldn't open the door. But

the maid had seen the taxi and she opened it so fast I fell in. I ran up the stairs without a word to her and I got into Mary's room. I was on the floor by the bed.

Mary opened her eyes and a little smile came on her lips. "I knew you would come back," she whispered.

The doctor said, "Every child has to have a little sickness—measles, mumps and so on. It wasn't your fault she got a bug, you can't keep her in cotton wool all her life. Brace up, now, Mary's fine. Too bad you haven't got six children."

If I had six, I'd be dead, I said. He said, I want you to let her run around with those little Irish kids in the alley, they're healthy as pigs. You wrap her up too much. She's a healthy child but she needs toughening.

So Mary tore around like a hoodlum for the next five years, climbing trees, playing baseball, digging caves, skating and bicycling.]

My daughter's ambition is to be a great actress.

[Maybe she has some talent. At first she used to make up little plays. "Mamma, I'm the Little Lord Jesus, you be the wise men and wisshop me. . . . Mamma, I'm an Indian Chief and I'm going to want your fox fur to trim my leggings. . . . Mamma, I'm going to be Joseph in the Christmas pageant at Sunday school, where can I get a beard?"

Then when the new dancing teacher came, Mary was going to be a dancer. She practiced hours before the mirror, and walked with a peculiar swinging gait that an-

noyed Ken a lot. He said it looked as if she might get unhinged any minute.

But after we went to the big football game, she wanted to be a football player. "Oh Mamma, why wasn't I a boy? I'd rather play left end than anything in the world. Boys have all the opportunities. It's dumb being a girl. I'd rather play end than be quarterback."

Maybe she could at least play in the band. So she borrowed a trombone from somewhere. She practiced a lot. Kenneth said, "Mary, does that instrument have any soft pedal? Couldn't you kind of quiet it down some?" "No," she said, "when you play a trombone you have to give, Papa." "A trombone sounds all right to me in a bunch of things, Ken said, but all by itself it's kind of melancholy. Maybe if you could play it on key, it would be more cheerful." "There you see, that's all the encouragement I get from my family." She was getting deep in the misunderstood stage.

Kenneth got her the riding tickets to take her mind off the trombone now and then. But then she wanted to run a livery stable. She wanted him to build over the sunroom for a horse stall. She said the house was big enough. We had moved to a big brick place at the edge of town. There was a garden and a bird bath and a game room. But there wasn't a stable. We had the horse question pretty hard but just as Kenneth got to wondering if we could put a horse in the garage and keep the sedan in the laundry, the famous poet came to lecture.

Poetry broke out like measles. Mary shut herself away and wrote poetry. Some of it was printed in the school magazine and Mary got to be editor that way. "Your daughter has a real gift for writing," all the teachers told

me, "*you must do all you can for her artistic future.*"
*Kenneth said he couldn't understand some of the poems.
They were kind of abstract. He said, "I hope she's not
going to take after my aunt Emily. She was a poet and
she went crazy." He said, "She used to run around town
carving things on the trees." He said, "Poetry isn't a
thing to get involved with. Didn't you tell me Emily
Dickinson used to lower a basket from her window for
her meals? How would you like it if Mary got to lower-
ing a basket from the bedroom window for her supper?
You better get her out with boys and girls more. Besides
if she's going to be a poet, she better begin hunting up
millionaires to support her.*"

*I said, "You can't thwart her. All the books on child
adjustment say it's bad to thwart them. I always wanted
to be a missionary, for instance, and my family wouldn't
hear of it." "A hell of a missionary you'd have made,"
said Ken. "Mamma, do you think I could be a poet?" She
was intense.*

*That was the only thing certain about her. She was
fiercely ardent about whatever it was she was doing. That
intensity was almost frightening. She never could take
things as they came along. She was never easy. Now she
was all dark grave eyes and sensitive mouth and her hair
was like a mist in her neck and there was always a book
in her hand.*

*I said, "Don't worry about it, Mary. If you're sup-
posed to be a poet, you will be."*

*"But Mamma, my life is a third over and I've got to
hurry! I'm almost fifteen! Look at Thomas Chatterton.
He was a great poet and already dead at seventeen. Look
at Keats—look at Shelley and Byron!"*

*I said weakly, "Well, Wordsworth lived quite a while,
didn't he?"*

*"Oh Wordsworth," she said, turning up her nose.
Since the Senior play she wants to be an actress.]*

My daughter's temperament and tastes are. . . .

*[Well, what are they? What is she like, really, under-
neath? Do I know her at all? Mothers can be lonely. I
know Mary wears her stockings through at the heel and
tears her slips at the shoulder. I know she won't eat cauli-
flower and is crazy about ripe olives. I've been right in
the house with her for sixteen years and now she is as
remote as polar ice. She withdraws into some world of
her own right while she is buttering her mashed potato
at supper. She leads a secret life, she is a person. Now and
then she looks down at me from some mountain top and
waves, I see awareness in her eyes. Then it is gone.*

*There was the party. Mary didn't want to go. But I
got her a new dress and an evening jacket. Kenneth and
I worried and worried over how to get a boy to ask her;
you can't just hire an escort. Kenneth thought he could
take her and Mary just burst into tears. "I'd be disgraced
for life," she said. "Do you want to disgrace me for life?"*

*Finally I had a brilliant idea. I gave a dinner party for
the whole class with the idea they could go on and dance
at the party afterward, in a clump. There were twenty
of them. We had three extra maids. The boys all stayed
in the study throwing pennies and the girls giggled in the
living room until dinner. Two of the boys got to wres-*

tling and broke my best Lalique vase. Mary had as much life as a soap carving. She just stood by the fire. Corinne Walker went boldly in with the boys and picked out the best-looking one, Wade Harmon, and got him to dancing with her in the hall. Mary just didn't make an effort.

What does a mother do when she is afraid her daughter will be socially unacceptable? Wring her hands and say, "Be charming? Make the boys like you?" You can teach Latin and History and trombone playing, but you can't teach sex appeal. It's there or it isn't. What had I done that I shouldn't have? Maybe she'd been a tomboy too long. Those Irish children—but that was for her health. Her health was fine.

She looked shy and serious and Corinne was laughing and kittening with Wade Harmon. I was lighting candles and my hands felt spatters of hot wax. I called them in and they fell on the dinner like wolves. The dining room looked like a wreck after they charged out. They began to pair off then, to go on to the party at the club. Mary stood by the stairway with her hand tight on the banister, she smiled a fixed smile. "Goodby, Perry, see you later. Sure, Billy, goodby, see you later. Glad you liked it, Corinne."

When there were only two more left, Mary gave me one look. I smiled brightly. Mary stiffened then and said, "Guess I'll mush on with you. Oh sure, c'mon, we'll be late."

The door slammed. I rushed to the phone and called Ken out of a board meeting for the new school. "Come home," I said, "I have got to go on to the dance. I can't stand it."

"Hey, woman, I'm working." "You come home

quick," I said. *"Oh all right,"* he said helplessly. *"Just hold everything."*

I got into a black dress. This was a dance I wasn't going to miss, but I didn't care whether I got on the floor or not. I brushed my hair and put on some makeup and walked up and down waiting for Kenneth.

"What's the matter?" he called as he came in. Then as he saw the house he whistled. *"You had the marines?"* he asked.

By the time he got his tux on it was late. We got to the club about ten. We came up on the porch and I said, *"Let's look in first, Ken."* My hands were cold.

The floor was crowded. The girls and boys looked young and gay, the girls wore shining frocks and flowers over their ears in the style. The dance music made a pattern of lovely rhythms. Corinne and Wade were at the punch bowl and she was lifting her face as she drank the pink stuff. It was an old trick, I used to do it, the light falls just right on lashes and cheeks and it makes a male feel protective, especially if you get the right softness on your mouth.

Mary was sitting beside an artificial palm with two other girls. Every time a boy walked that way, she bent her head and looked at the floor as if something important were there. Her mouth was carved in a smile and her eyes when she did look up were like the eyes of a wounded wild bird.

"Well, let's go on in," said Kenneth.

"Oh no, we can't. I guess we can't go in."

"Are you crazy? You got me out of an important meeting and into these damned clothes and now you want to go home."

"Oh Kenneth, Mary will never forgive us if she knows we came."

"Then what's the idea of coming at all?"

"I thought if she were having a grand rush—but the way it looks, Mary's so proud."

"Why can't we go in and take her home if she's not having a good time? I'll get her."

"No. Ken, it's like the law of the jungle. We can't help her. I guess maybe," I said slowly, "maybe you've got to run with the pack, and learn it somehow."

We went on home. I sat up in the living room holding a book and listening. It was a cool moonlit night, an April night. Trees were misting with buds, and the sky was heavy with young stars. Dance music came in over the radio, sweet and dreamy and then hot and rackety with swing. Kenneth sat up a while and then went on to bed.

I kept going to the window and looking down the moonlit street. I got out my basket and mended her slips where the straps were pulled out. I emptied all the ashtrays and straightened the pillows on the sofa. I looked out.

She came down the street alone, walking with her head up. Her face was frozen in that smile. She walked fast, almost running, but when she got to the front walk she slowed, and came creeping softly to the door.

I had my head over the book again as she came in. I said lightly, "Oh hello, Mary."

"Hello, Mamma." She spoke carefully. "Thank you for the dinner, it was very nice." Her face had that shut secret look.

"Did you—have a good time at the dance?"

"Oh yes, I had a good time."

If I could have comforted her, eased the hurt! Or let her know I understood.

"Goodnight, Mamma."

She hurried upstairs and closed her door. Shutting out the alien world.

I turned out the lights and went up too. I could hear through her shut door the long strangling sobs. But I couldn't help her.

Two weeks later she came home from school with Wade Harmon and when I was passing by the living room I saw her lifting a cup of hot chocolate for him. She looked up at him with a soft little smile. The afternoon light fell on her long amber lashes and on the curve of her cheek. Wade was looking protective.

At supper she said, "I'm going with Wade to the next dance. I'm going to change the way I do my hair," she added.

Kenneth's jaw fell open and I said very quickly, "What dress will you wear?" I stepped on what I thought was his foot under the table but it was the buzzer and the maid flew in.

"More coffee," I said.

"The pot's full, Ma'am," she answered.

Mary said dreamily, "I'll wear the green. Green is Wade's favorite color."

Kenneth burst out, "How did he happen to ask you? Why, only two weeks ago—ouch," he finished, glaring at me. It was the foot that time.

Mary gave him a feminine and disarming smile. "Oh," she said gently, "I just happened to drop a note to one of the girls and he happened to find it and read it. So he wanted to know why I thought he was handsomer than

Clark Gable and a better athlete than the Iowa Sledge-hammer."

"Now Mary, you don't mean to say you think that pimple-faced . . ."

"Corinne was telling him he was kind of like Leslie Howard," Mary continued pleasantly. "He doesn't admire Leslie Howard because he wears glasses."

That was in May. On December 24, her birthday, Mary came in while I was buttering the breakfast toast. She had an apricot breakfast coat on and her hair drawn back from her forehead in the new way. She was slim and softly rounded and the childish look was gone from her big dark eyes but somehow her nose still looked childish to me. Her mouth was intense. I knew that intense tight look. But I couldn't think what it was. I said happily, "Such a beautiful day for your birthday! I thought we might do the Christmas last minutes this morning. I forgot Aunt Caroline and she's so fussy."

Mary nibbled an edge of toast. "I promised Wade I'd go out with him," she said. "A bunch of us are going someplace. Wassail, Mamma. Send Aunt Car a magazine subscription, it's so easy."

I said, "Mary, your father feels you ought to go out with different boys. You've been out every night this vacation with Wade."

Her face got hard as an icicle. She said harshly, "Why can't you let me alone ever?"

"Why Mary," I said, "I only meant . . ."

But she was gone. I started after her and then noticed she managed to eat two pieces of toast and drink her orange juice and milk and get away with three slices of bacon, just in that delicate way. Her stomach was all *right. She'd been up too late nights. It made her edgy.*

I heard Wade's auto horn and thought I should ask if he had a heater in the car and chains on. But I didn't. It made the children so mad to be questioned. They were always trying to be free—suddenly I remembered that was the way I had felt. Before Mary was born. I had wings too. Once. Sixteen—nearly seventeen—years ago.

So when Mary whisked past me in her squirrel jacket I called, "Have a good time, darling."

She checked her mad speed and said, "I may bring Wade for dinner. Could you have duckling? He loves it."

It began to snow at noon. Going to be a blizzard, said the butcher as I ordered the duckling. I had so many errands I had to go downtown after lunch. The streets were deep with snow and the street trucks already were frantically swallowing it up. Christmas lights shone, holly and mistletoe on the sidewalks made mounds of white. Everybody staggered against the drifts with arms thick with packages for the forgotten relatives. My hands were so cold in the ermine mittens, I went into the drugstore to warm up.

"Terrible storm, I'd hate to be out in it," said the druggist. "Hasn't been such a snow for sixteen years. I remember the date because my nephew got stalled in the country that day. Him and his wife wound up the windows and turned the motor on to keep warm. They both died of monoxide gas. Road shovelers found them dead. I don't know why folks will shut the windows like that."

I said, "Give me some aspirin, I'm aching all over."

"You got to watch the flu," he said, "this is flu weather."

I went out and it was dusk, the snow was a dusk all

of its own, thick and silent, falling and falling from a close thick sky. It was cold, too.

When I got home, Mary wasn't there. She ought to have been back long ago, wrapping her things for the tree. I could smell the duckling, a brown smell as if it should be out of the oven. Ken was listening to the radio report of the weather.

"Hey, where's Mary?" he asked. "Say, this is a real old-time blizzard, the trains aren't running. What do you know?"

I said, "Mary and Wade went out right after breakfast."

"Where?"

"She didn't say."

"They'll be along. But she ought to be here."

The phone rang. I ran to answer it. It was Mrs. Harmon and her voice was thin and taut over the wire. "Where's Wade?"

Well, I didn't know. She was nearly frantic, she said. Wade was supposed to be home by two-thirty to take the Christmas basket to the orphan's home, and he knew the orphans had their things Christmas Eve.

I tried to quiet her down, and she rang off at last. The maid came in and said dinner was practically ruined, so I said we would have to eat. I ran upstairs to wash my face and hands. There was nothing to worry about. But Mary always came in on time, she was good that way. And the weather was frightful and then too it was Christmas Eve. All the families in our crowd were having their family suppers, the children conceded Christmas Eve to their parents, and Easter Sunday. So there wouldn't be a last-minute dance at the club or anything.

No harm calling the club to be sure. I called on the

upstairs phone. Nobody was at the club except the staff getting ready for a banquet.

As I went past Mary's room, I stopped to close her window. Snow lay deep on the sill, the curtains dragging with it. I stopped to wipe it up with a bath towel. Then I saw the draught had blown open Mary's little blue diary that she kept on her desk. There was the date, December 24, and under it a single hasty line.

"Nothing matters except that we love each other."

I sank onto the bed, pressing my knees together. Maybe I had felt they were serious, but it looked different, written down that way. There was a quality of feeling in that simple line. It could mean—almost anything. At the thought of all it could mean, I beat my hands together. How could I know? What should I think? Something was ringing in my head, I tried to push the sound away, and then I understood it was the phone.

Mrs. Harmon was on the wire and she was frantic. "I've phoned all over town," she said hoarsely, "absolutely everywhere. I even called all the ice cream parlors and the movies. They just aren't—anywhere. Not anywhere!"

My hands were shaking. I said, "We'll hear soon."

"I don't see why you let your daughter go off without telling you," she said; and I answered sharply, "I assumed she was all right with your son."

Kenneth called, "Now don't you mothers start fighting like a couple of hens."

I got him upstairs and showed him the diary and his face went white. "You don't think—you don't think they —no, of course not. Absurd. Come and eat your dinner, they'll be in any minute."

"But where are they?" I asked. He didn't answer.

We choked down a few mouthfuls of burned duckling. Of course they could have driven over the state line. If that was what they meant. Mary was just sixteen. She was so intense about everything.

About nine-thirty we couldn't stand it, just waiting. Kenneth got the car out and we drove out. Kenneth wanted to get the police, but then he said we better wait a little longer, publicity was a mess. All the lights were glowing all over town, and the snow was lessening a little. No taxis were running, the busses had stopped. But the carolers came down the street singing, "God rest you merry gentlemen, let nothing you dismay."

Kenneth took the main road from town, but ran head on into a snow drift. When he backed again, he said, "I'm going to call the traffic men. You know, they might be stuck somewhere."

"Oh Kenneth—would they shut the car and leave the motor running?" That was a new terror. Kenneth said, "Don't think about it."

The snow plows were out, the men said, and they were opening up the roads as fast as possible. Now the snow was letting up, they'd have everything clear before dawn. They'd tow in any stalled folks.

Before dawn!

We went home again and had hot coffee. Then Kenneth said he was going back uptown and try to ride out with the road men. He'd phone me. He kissed me and said, "Keep your chin up, lady."

I walked up and down in the empty house. I thought of everything, and it all happened in my heart. The minister saying, do you take this man—and Mary, her face fresh and cold with snow saying trustingly, I do. A cheap hotel or a heated tourist cabin near Bayside. Or the closed car and snow drifting on the runningboard and Mary and Wade holding hands. Or maybe they hadn't meant marriage. Maybe they didn't mean that. You could annul a marriage, but you couldn't annul memory. If Mary gave up her young grave chastity, nobody could turn the clock back. She'd be changed. Maybe some girls could take it as a matter of course, but Mary wasn't like that.

Mary was always serious.

I began again. The way she looked at him, with a kind of soft wonder. The way he put on her coat, as if his hands loved to touch the fabric that warmed her young slim body. The way they laughed at secret jokes.

I must have failed. I pushed her into this boy-and-girl game, myself. Trying to adjust her socially. Then I'd been so blind. I could have forbidden him to come—taken her away—talked to her—oh no, I couldn't. Mothers were helpless. All those old foolish things parents tried never really protected their children.

"Please God," I said, "please, please not Mary. Not yet."

The house was deathly cold and finally I turned the thermostat up. I roused the fire in the fireplace. I put on an old chenille robe. I knew death must come cold like that in the reluctant bones.

Dawn made a faint smear in the grey sky. Then the whole pure snowy world took on a faint light of its own. I pushed the curtains aside and stared out, my eyes hot and the lids tight.

A milk truck labored down the street. It stopped before our house.

Mary and Wade got out, and waved to the driver and ran up the steps. I couldn't move. I stood like stone as they burst in.

Mary said, "Why, Mamma, what are you doing up at this hour? Were you worried?"

"Worried," I said. "Oh, Mary."

"We're starved, can we eat something?" She was flinging off her things. "Wait till I tell you—oh, Mamma it was so exciting!"

"Exciting," I said faintly.

She said, "We went out to see if we could get a bunch of cedar from the swamp, and what do you think, it stormed so we were stuck fast! Weren't we, Wade?"

"I'll say we were," he laughed, "the old bus like to sunk down to China."

"Go up and wash, you're pig dirty," Mary said to him. "I'll scramble some eggs in a minute."

"What's that in your scarf?"

"You'll be surprised," she said. She brought it over, still talking. "So we found a farmhouse," she said, "and the wires were all down so we just had to leave the car forever! And we played backgammon all night and look— he had these darling beagle puppies so Wade bought me one for my Christmas!"

She unrolled the scarf and there was a small shivering puppy about the size of a pint milkbottle. Mary said, "Isn't he perfect? And the marvelous thing is we were going to get a dog anyway, we decided last night we couldn't wait any longer. And here this very farmer had beagles! Isn't it amazing the way things work out?"

"Yes," I said, "it's amazing. Mary, your father's out hunting you."

"*We met him. He'll be along soon as he gets the car go-ing,*" *she said.*

"*Mary, I thought—I was so afraid—and Mrs. Harmon thought you were—you and Wade—had run away to—had eloped.*"

Her mouth fell open. "*My goodness, Mamma,*" *she said,* "*whatever would put such an idea in your head? Wade said his mother would have a fit but I said you would figure out that we couldn't phone on account of the storm but we could look out for ourselves O.K.*"

"*Well,*" *I said,* "*it looked—different from this end.*"

Mary yelled up the stairs, "*Wade, phone your mother. She thinks we ran away to get married!*"

The puppy began to whimper and Mary put it up in her neck. She kissed it. She said, "*You ought to know I wouldn't trick you, Mamma. Besides when we get married we want to have a real wedding. You get presents then.*"

She smiled at me over the wobbling puppy head. "*You wouldn't really worry, would you, Mamma?*" *she asked.* "*Look, wouldn't it be a good idea to raise beagles?*"]

Miss Elizabeth Winthrop
Dean of Women
State University
Monongahela

My dear Miss Winthrop:

I have your letter asking me to write you about my daughter, frankly, freely and objectively.

My daughter Mary is sixteen. Her birthday is December 24. Her health is excellent. My daughter's ambition is to be a great actress. Her temperament and tastes are those of the average sixteen-year-old girl.

I feel sure she will adjust satisfactorily to the University, and will not be a trouble. She has never given me cause to worry.

Sincerely,
Mary March
(Mrs. Kenneth March)

Just
a Little Havoc

❁❁❁❁❁❁❁❁❁❁❁❁   ❁

There is no reason for a girl to have trouble making up her mind which man she wants to marry. It is perfectly obvious that one man is the right one, and she should know it. Bill told Sally so; in fact, if he told her once, he told her a thousand times. Besides, he said, no girl could marry a man named Ernest. "Show me a single magazine," he said, "in which a girl marries Ernest."

But Sally said it was his parents' fault, as Bill's red hair was due to his mother. "And I've read a lot of articles lately," she said, "about not just getting married on the basis of romantic attraction. You fill out charts and things: Do you like company? Are you jealous? Do you have the same interests?"

"Look," said Bill; "you and me, we aren't an article. We're us."

"For instance," said Sally, "do we really have enough in common?"

"We both like you pretty well."

"Don't be silly. I mean it seriously. Like Ravel's *Bolero* and Thomas Wolfe and fried onions."

"The *Bolero* is all right," said Bill, "but Thomas Wolfe is a mistake on your part—he's too wordy. Your taste in literature is so spotty; in fact, it's just plain collegiate."

"See what I mean?" said Sally, getting red. "Ernest thinks I'm perfect."

"Ernest is a man without a spine," said Bill.

They made up several days later and went for a drive. Bill cleverly brought into the conversation everything they had in common. He loved her dreadfully, and he would have years after they were married to cure her of liking Dean Martin better than Frank Sinatra, and Swiss cheese better than Bleu. But now, he had to erase the horrid effect of the hue and cry about marriage. For, he admitted it, if you read all the articles and all the speeches and all the books on psychiatry, you would never dare marry at all. The dice were always against you.

"What do you want for your birthday?" he asked. "Besides the engagement ring, I mean."

"Ernest wants to give me a ring, too," said Sally. "And he is giving me a pair of carved ivory figurines. They are exquisite."

Bill groaned. Ernest had a lot of money. Given him by those same people who gave him the name. Bill had $250 a week; and a raise eventually when he moved up a peg in the architectural firm.

Bill said now, "Darling, I'd like to give you the Milky Way set in pieces of the sky. But what do you really want? Is there anything you have always wanted and never had?"

He drove more slowly. Sally began to think, her blue eyes dreamy. Suddenly she pointed to the side of the road and said, "There! Stop, Bill; that's what I've always wanted!"

"What?" He stopped obediently. Suppose she wanted that lovely old white house set in the sugar maples?

Then he saw the sign: IRISH SETTER PUPPIES FOR SALE.

"That's what I want," said Sally. "An Irish setter."

Bill said, "But, darling, I've got two cockers, and they are yours, too—or will be when we get married."

"A setter," said Sally, leaning her cheek on her hand, "the gentlest, noblest, most beautiful, most serene—a setter is like a poem. An Irish setter, the color of maple leaves in autumn—a noble head, a sensitive personality—oh, Bill!"

Bill stopped the car and got out and went around and opened the door for her. "You have named your poison," he said.

There were thirteen puppies in the pen, some tawny, some fire-wagon red, some burnished copper. They were a mass of legs and tails. Their faces were all eager.

"Good heavens!" said Bill. "How does anyone cope with a litter that size? When Penny had six we were floored."

Sally was hanging over the fence, her soft hair blowing in the wind. "I'll take that one!" she said, pointing.

"Which one? They all look alike to me," said Bill. "Now, with a cocker, they're all different."

"That one right there," said Sally. "Look at her sweet, gentle, noble face!"

"Do they all have eight legs?" asked Bill.

He tried to get the one she wanted. "No, the other one," said Sally. The trouble was, as fast as he got one, four more were there, too. Finally Sally managed to hold the girl of her choice.

"But if you put her down again, we'll have it all over," said Bill.

Sally whipped out her lipstick and made a nice X in the middle of the fat stomach. "Now let's go buy her," she said.

Kathleen Mavourneen rode home in Sally's lap, which she filled comfortably. She sat very still, very grave, saying nothing. At eleven weeks she was just a nice size to cuddle. Sally cuddled.

"Oh, Bill, you don't know what you've done for me," said Sally blissfully. "I'm going to be so happy with her!"

"She may be a little trouble," said Bill doubtfully.

"Nonsense," said Sally. "Look at you with two—they aren't a bit of bother." She added, "A setter is no trouble at all." She kissed the dark-red head the way Bill wished she would kiss him. "She's just my precious red rose," said Sally sentimentally.

"Now, how about setting the date for a wedding?" urged Bill, striking while the iron was sizzling.

Sally said, "Bill, I guess I do love you. Only—I told Ernest I wouldn't make a final decision until I see him again tomorrow night. I've got to be fair to Ernest." She said, "And oh, Bill, he does need me so much."

"And I don't, I suppose."

Bill did feel sorry for Ernest. But not half as sorry as he would feel for himself if he lost Sally.

"I won't even phone until Sunday," he said nobly.

He didn't, either. One reason was that he came down

with a heavy case of flu, which may or may not have been an act of God. It gave Ernest a clear field for ten days and gave Bill lots of time to reflect on just how nice a guy Ernest was besides having so many material advantages like houses and sports cars and elaborate stereo sets.

The first day Bill was up, Sally came over with Kathleen.

"Maybe it's my fever," said Bill, "but did you exchange her for an older dog?"

"Certainly not," said Sally; "she's just growing."

"That's understatement," said Bill. "I wonder if she is part pony."

"Bill, I've got to go to Texas," said Sally. "My eighty-year-old aunt has sent for me. She wants to settle her property, and I'm the only relative she trusts."

"I'll go with you," said Bill. "It can be part of the honeymoon."

"You've got to stay here," said Sally. "You're supposed to work for a living."

"I've got another week off."

"The point is," said Sally, looking soft and sweet, "I thought you'd take care of Kathleen. She can just move in with Penny and Moonlight. It makes it simple."

Bill looked at Kathleen. She came over and got on his lap. A few legs hung over the edge of the chair and her chin rested on the arm, but her main portion was really on his lap. Her tail waved and tickled his left ear.

"Why doesn't Ernest take her?" he asked.

"Ernest doesn't love her," said Sally; "Ernest says she is a nuisance. She's cutting teeth, Bill, and you know they do chew when they are teething."

"Yes, I do know."

"So it wasn't her fault it was Ernest's best trousers."

"Definitely not. But what were they doing at your house?"

"Oh, Ernest was in them," she said.

"I'll take her," said Bill.

"I'll be right back," Sally promised, "in two or three weeks. And then we'll settle everything."

When she left, Bill looked at Kathleen. He didn't have Sally but he did have her dog. "Quite a lot of dog," he said.

Bill had a house, fortunately, and a nice, fenced yard for his cockers. And a Dutch door between the back room and the kitchen, so they could be shut out when necessary. So it really wouldn't be any trouble to have a third dog for a while.

He let Penny and Miss Moonlight into the house, and Kathleen bounded over to welcome them by swinging wildly on their ears. Penny growled and Moon bit her. Kathleen screamed and fell on her back, paws held helplessly up in the air. Her eyes were sadder than a tragedy queen.

Bill explained to the cockers. "Redhead is a guest. You must be very kind and polite to her. She is sensitive, you can see that."

Kathleen bounded up and strode toward him, tail waving. He noticed that she could walk right over a standing cocker, and it made the cocker give the curious effect of being a trundle bed under a four-poster.

The first day, Bill was pretty busy. He put the three dogs in the yard. Redhead loped around waving her amiable tail, and then leaped lightly over the fence.

Penny and Moon did not follow, so she jumped back and urged them on. Penny tried hard, and fell back and twisted a tendon, and limped for a week. Moon landed on the return trip in the barberry bush and got three hours of briers in her show coat.

In the end, Redhead had to open the gate for them, which she managed by jumping onto the latch. They all three set out for parts unknown.

Bill was trying to match up the fourteen rubbers Redhead had retrieved from the upper front hall closet and he missed this the first time. But he did hear the phone ring.

"Bill, your dogs are over here," said Beth Basset, "and they've got a setter with them. They're all worn out. What is the matter?"

"Be right over," said Bill. "Keep them in."

They had covered considerable waterfront somewhere and were three very sodden dogs when he got them home. By the time they were cleaned up and de-briered and dry, it was suppertime.

"I guess it's the kennel run for you, Redhead," he said. He put down three bowls of food, double for Kathleen, and sat down to his own modest meal. Bill ate at home when he was there, and he was a fair cook. The cleaning woman kept the pans washed up.

He turned to pour his coffee, and when he turned back, a red muzzle rested eagerly at the edge of his plate. Redhead was tall enough so she could rest her elbows on the table and really take part in the meal. Bill shut her in the back room for discipline and sat down again to cut his meat.

Kathleen came right back over the Dutch door. She climbed, using her front legs and sliding her body up, then lunging down. As an athletic feat, it was stupendous.

Bill put her back, and shut the top half of the door, too.

He took a couple of bites, and then noticed the door swing slowly open. Someone was coming in.

"Who's there?" he called.

Kathleen's noble head appeared, she took her paw from the latch, and entered, pleasantly placing her nose by his plate again.

"Now, look here," said Bill: "this is too much. You get down and *stay* down!"

He was a little tired. He began to gulp his dinner, between times putting the dog down.

But when he won out, she sat and looked at him with such agonized suffering that he couldn't enjoy a single bite.

Penny and Moon were munching dog biscuits in the study when he broke down and gave Redhead a piece of lamb chop, but they heard it, all right, so he had to divide up the rest of the meat. All three helped eat up everything else he had cooked.

When he went to answer the phone again, Redhead took his plate, too, and tucked it away behind a sofa cushion. She carried it without chipping, with a soft, bird-dog mouth, but it took him a while to locate it, not having a bird-dog nose himself.

"All right," he said to her, "I'll take care of you until Sally gets back, then that is the end. You go to a boarding kennel for good."

He put the dogs all out while he got ready for bed. He was still shaky from his fever. He would get into bed with a new mystery and have a nice rest.

His bedroom was on the first floor, and he came back downstairs after taking all the pink and green footballs the doctor prescribed, and turned on the reading lamp and got into bed. He left the windows open two feet or so. Penny and Moon would play half an hour or so and then bark at the back door.

The bed felt wonderful to his aching bones. He turned the first page and settled back. Then he heard a noise, and looked up. There was a face at the window by the bed.

It was the face of Kathleen Mavourneen. Standing on tiptoe, she rested her chin on the sill and looked at him thoughtfully. Muddy paws clung to the clean white paint.

"Now, look," said Bill; "you go play. Run all around."

A look of exquisite pleasure came into her eyes at his voice. Her mouth opened in a happy smile. The next minute she bounded in happily and flung herself on him, together with a good deal of garden dirt.

"Blast and fury!" swore Bill, tangled up with those long legs.

A page parted from its hold on the back of the book and fluttered away. Kathleen began hopping up and down on the bed, positively radiant.

Bill got up. He let Penny and Moon in. He had an extra cocker bed in the cellar, and he went down and brought it up.

"That's yours," he said. "Get in it."

Kathleen got in. A good deal of her hung over the edges of the bed but she loved it. She lovingly bit off a corner and munched it.

Bill shut them all in the back room and went back to bed. Then they began to play games, the three of them.

Kathleen began to bark, a deep, mannish bark. Penny joined in with her slight feminine squeal, and Moon got hysterical. Bill shut his eyes and tried to sleep.

He fell into a heavy doze and turned over. But he seemed to be crowded in his bed, and definitely the bed was humping around. He opened his eyes again. Three were in bed with him. Kathleen had lifted the latch and they all had come in.

Bill groaned and got up again.

He went down cellar once more and found a large hook and eye like the one the dog-run gate was fastened with. Shuddering only a little, he screwed it into the priceless batten door, put the three back in their room, and hooked the big hook securely.

And went to bed again and dreamed he was living with an Arabian pony. . . .

The cleaning woman came the next week, on Saturday. Her name was Belle, and she was a widow who took care of a number of neighbors to eke out her pension. She made very fine pies, and usually did a roast for Bill and a batch of light rolls and left them on the table covered with a clean cloth.

Bill was out doing errands when she came, the three dogs with him. He had a lot of things to get—shoes and shoe laces and a couple of sofa cushions. Then two rugs had jagged tears in them and had to be mended.

He got back around noon, and left the dogs in the car while he carried the eggs and butter and milk and some of the packages in.

Belle met him at the door.

"Good morning, Belle, and how are you?" asked Bill.

"Very well, thank you," she said. "Mr. Brewster, I am giving notice as of today."

Bill dropped everything and stared wildly at her. "But what's the matter?" he cried.

"I have my reputation to consider," she said, "and I don't care to work in any place where there are such goings-on as there are in your house, Mr. Brewster."

"Goings-on? What do you mean? You mean because I've had flu?"

"You know what I mean," said Belle, more in sorrow than in anger. "Drunken orgies."

"But I haven't had any drunken orgies!" Bill cried again.

"Do you expect me to believe that?" she asked, eying him sternly. "Would a man sober and in his right senses put all his shoes and slippers on the mantel? I ask you honestly, would he?"

Bill gasped.

"Furthermore," she said, "there is a pair of galoshes on your bureau, and the candlesticks that belong on the low table are in your bathroom on top of the medicine cabinet. And, as if that were not enough," she added, "there are those hooks and eyes on all the good doors!"

"Let me explain," said Bill.

"Then your best dressing gown," she went on; "somebody has been cutting it up, and one window shade is shredded. And somebody who couldn't see where he was going has fallen in the coal hod and got coal all over the living-room floor."

"Look, Belle," said Bill; "it's just the dog!"

"Dog!" she sniffed. "I've been doing for you all the time and I know those innocent little dogs of yours. They wouldn't throw mud all over the windowpanes, not they!" She said, "I have cleaned up, and there's a small rib roast in the kitchen."

Kathleen was bored sitting in the car by now, so she pried at the front window, from which the snap button was gone. She got out and loped in the back door, paused long enough to gather up the roast and cantered in to Bill, happy as a bride the sun shines on.

"There she is," said Bill. "There's my drunken orgy."

Belle screamed, which hurt Kathleen's feelings. She laid the roast on Bill's lap and lay down on her back, paws helpless, eyes obviously filled with tears.

"You see," said Bill; "she's sensitive. You've hurt her dreadfully."

Kathleen sat up, dolorous but dignified now, leaned on her crossed forepaws, and languished at Belle.

"Why, the poor, sweet baby," cried Belle. "She wouldn't do a thing!"

"Hang around the rest of the day," said Bill, "and see what you see."

Dignified also, he went out and got Penny and Moon. When he came back, Kathleen was trying to sit on Belle's lap to be comforted. He noticed she was twice as big as yesterday.

He went back to work on Monday, so Sunday he had to make a new bed for Kathleen. Longer and wider. She helped carry the two-by-fours, and also brought the best satin sofa pillow to add to it.

Bill said, "I know you don't mean to be a bother; you can't help it," and she almost fainted with joy at the words.

One thing was, he said to himself, she was still a baby, and yet so amazingly large. Young cockers got into trouble, too, but in a small way. Everything Kathleen did, she did in a big way. When she waved her tail, it waved over the whole room. When she took tacks from the love seat, she got a whole row out at once. And small objects were just bite-size to her.

And then she was so gay, so high-spirited, but when he disciplined her, she collapsed in a miserable heap. He found it hard to punish her when she hid her head in her arms and sobbed piteously.

"No," he said, "you just aren't practical, and Sally has to realize it."

She came in just then carrying her feeding pan in a suggestive manner. So he stopped working to fix her another of those endless meals.

How wonderful it would be when Sally got home and they put Kathleen in a nice boarding kennel—and they'll have to have a fence as high as the Cliffs of Dover, he added, to keep her in.

His own dog pen was useless. She would go in joyously with Penny and Moon and play with them an hour or so, then leap over the top, and come out. If she got lonesome, she went back in.

Yes, the house would be so peaceful and quiet and ordered when Kathleen was gone. And he wouldn't have to stumble over bones and bits of firewood any more, either. He might even get time to read a little in the evening when he was not with Sally.

Kathleen had her own box of toys by now, those he bought for her and remnants of his hand-woven scarf and knitted slippers she had chosen for herself. It was a fine idea; she would mull them over, pick out the toy of the moment, toss it in the air, pounce on it with the floor shaking, put it down, and go hunting for something new, like an ashtray.

They made a beautiful sight, you had to admit, said Bill, when they all went after a rabbit. Kathleen ranged ahead, with her long, lovely leaps, and the sturdy little cockers skimmed along behind, ears lying on the wind like wings. If she got too far ahead, she ran with her head turned over her shoulder to be sure they were coming.

The third week, Sally wired she was coming home, and please would Bill come to the airport to meet her.

Belle, thoroughly resigned by now, cleaned the house and cooked all kinds of delicacies so Bill could have a nondrunken party. She ranged the food on the top of shelves and inside the oven with the door closed. The best sofa cushions were stacked on top of the radio. The cigarettes were on top of the mantel. Everything was ready.

The plane was due at six-thirty in the evening, so Bill left the office early, went home, fed the dogs, dressed. Then he dashed back to get some flowers. As the door banged behind him, he heard Kathleen's low moan of sorrow.

"Well," said Bill to himself, "this is the last of that." He was whistling *Come Back to Erin, Mavourneen, Mavourneen,* but he thought, *Go Back*, instead of *Come Back*.

He felt fine. He had gotten rather thin chasing after the visiting firewoman, but he had a new suit, a very sharp tie and shirt, and Sally was coming. He would bring her home, here where she belonged. The fire was ready to light, the welcoming guests were invited to arrive half an hour later, so he could see Sally alone for a little while first.

"I want yellow freesias and white narcissus," he said,

"and a brown orchid; the first two for the table, the last with ribbon to wear." He'd remembered her favorites.

"I'm so sorry," said the florist, "we just sold the last freesia and the last orchid. Mr. Ernest Crowninfield took them."

Bill went wild. But it didn't matter, he had to take a gardenia and a bunch of daisies. He drove back to the house through two red lights. He would have to get to the airport first, grab Sally, and whisk her away.

Then the sobering thought struck him. She had wired Ernest, too! He groaned as he slammed the car door and ran into the house with his flowers. He didn't notice the back door was open, but when he got in he did notice that Kathleen was not there.

Penny and Moon were asleep under the range. Bill dropped the flowers and ran to the door and called. Then he rushed out into the yard and called louder.

Then he came back and hunted all over the house, even in the closets.

Then he faced the fact: She had run away, heaven knew where. He would miss the plane, Ernest would be there, it was a wonderful home-coming for Ernest.

But here he was, and Kathleen was out in the twilight, heedless, excitable, and running like a gazelle. He raced to the car, and drove around the nearest mile of streets, honking the horn [for she knew it perfectly] and leaning out to shout every three minutes.

And all the time a cold sickness rose in him. Sally would never forgive him. But over and above that dreadful emotion was the terrible fear for Kathleen.

She was so friendly, she loved the world. Anybody could steal her; he would not see her again. She was gone indeed. Or she was lying by the roadside, mangled. Skipping across the road to greet a passing car, and a hit-and-run motorist crashing into those delicate lovely legs, that sensitive muzzle.

The sun was setting and it was redder than blood. He turned the car back to the house, his hands shaking on the wheel. Better call the police and get them mobilized. Then he'd got out again.

He was talking to himself in a thick, muttering tone as he ran again to the house: "Sally darling, oh, my darling, I never meant—Redhead, where are you? I'm coming—if I only knew where. . . ."

He rushed to his room. But the door would not open. He wrenched at the knob and it turned, all right, but the door had not budged.

Then he heard a squeaking like a rusty hinge. He stopped, paralyzed. For whenever Kathleen woke up from a nap and yawned, her yawn was ended in exactly that long, rusty squeak.

"Redhead!" he shouted.

Somebody flung against the other side of the door.

There she was, inside his room. With the rest of his clothes, too. Now it came to him what had happened. She had gone in the window, bounded playfully around, and hit the door, letting that nice, heavy hook fall into its nice, solid eye. In other words, she was locked inside.

She barked happily and lunged at the door again.

"I'm coming!" shouted Bill. "Just sit still! I'm coming!"

She wailed. She was lonesome.

Bill ran out and went to the window. Kathleen's face peered out at him with love and interest. He tried to open the window, but that, of course, had a neat little spring catch inside. He ran down-cellar and got the crowbar and pried, and got a few slivers in his hands.

Kathleen was increasingly lonesome. She began to claw the panes. She barked. Penny and Moon went to the living room and barked, too, just to be in on things.

The plane was due in ten minutes now, but Bill was in the cellar again, getting screwdrivers and a hammer. Then he ran back to the window and took off the side frames, got the window itself out on the grass.

Kathleen fell out, a fragment of his tie on one ear. She was delirious with joy.

"So this is where you are," said a voice over his shoulder.

Bill looked around Kathleen's ear, and there was Sally.

"You wouldn't even meet me!" she said, and her voice was trembling, "and not a word, either!"

Bill wiped the grass and sticks out of his hair and laid down the hammer. "I was busy," he said, "Kathleen. . . ."

"Oh," said Sally, "oh, how is my darling red rose?" She held out her arms.

Kathleen waved a polite flag of greeting, but stayed where she was, half of her on Bill's knee, so he couldn't get up very easily.

"Your darling red rose," said Bill, "your darling red rose."

He got up then, and Kathleen sat on his foot, and looked up at him with passionate adoration.

Bill looked down. He was boiling like a caldron with all kinds of emotions, and he made a terrible effort to get them under control. But he had been through a good deal and he was overwrought.

"You can have Ernest if you want him," he said. "I am all through playing cat-and-mouse. For good."

Sally was suddenly pale, her eyes wide and frightened. "You—don't love me any more!" she whispered.

"I love you like the devil," he said, "but you can't have your cake and eat it too. This is the last time I ever ask you to marry me, and it's not some day or next year or next June. It's next Tuesday. That's my day off."

"Why—Bill. . . ."

"And I may as well tell you," he said fiercely, "you can take your choice between Ernest and me, but you can't have Kathleen—unless you do take me."

Sally said, "Bill, are you all right? What do you mean? And what are you doing with that window out of your bedroom?"

Bill dropped his hand, and Kathleen kissed it.

"And what do you mean I can't have Kathleen? She's my dog!"

"Not any more," said Bill firmly. "She belongs to me. By—right of eminent domain. I," he said grandly, "am training her. She needs me." He looked at Sally, and her mouth was beginning to curve.

"As for that"—he waved at the window—"she liked to go in and out that way."

"Bill," said Sally, "do you love me—still?"

"Sally," said Bill, "are you or are you not going to marry me?"

She flung herself into his arms. "Oh, Bill, I knew when I got out of the plane and there was nobody there but Ernest! I knew nobody mattered except you—always."

While he kissed her, Kathleen sat with her forepaws folded, her eyes slanted wistfully to the ground, her tail moving. Butter would never have melted in her mouth.

"I know I can make you happy," murmured Bill, after a long silence, "even if we never have a lot of money."

"It's going to be wonderful," sighed Sally dreamily. "And, besides, it doesn't cost so very much."

"What doesn't cost so very much?"

"Raising Irish setters," said Sally.

When the
Wood Grows Dry

✿✿✿✿✿✿✿✿✿✿✿✿   ✿

Miss Minerva Martin had been teaching voice at the college for more years than anyone could remember. She had simply been there since time began, weathering as the gray stone walls weathered under the insistent ivy. Presumably she was young once, and she must have had some kind of training; but in the early days when she came to Buckley, requirements were extremely fluid. She made references to study in Paris and Berlin and Milan, but possibly she had only been to the opera in Milan and never sung there. In any case, it was years and years ago.

She had only one real claim to glory. She had, in her narrow dark room at the top of the curlicues in Main Hall, a framed portrait of Hilda Larsen as a young girl; and whenever she had an opportunity, she told about being Hilda Larsen's friend and teacher before Hilda left the confines of Snowshoe, Minnesota, and went on to "singing like a reincarnation of Jenny Lind," as the critics said.

She never really came right out with a flat statement, but it was pretty clear that she had discovered Hilda. Hilda had a good voice, she did admit, and after some work on tone placement—"just the kind of work I want you to do, Cora Lee. . . ."

The portrait was of a young, thin Swedish girl with a ribbon around her hair, and a white shirtwaist and skirt. It was faded a little. It hung over the flat-topped student desk and was the only decoration in the room except for a china vase of dusty pampas grass which someone had once sent Miss Minerva from Florida.

On the desk a scrapbook of newspaper clippings was generally open. The clippings were of two kinds: clippings about Hilda Larsen; and clippings about student recitals at college. Nobody but Cora Lee had ever looked through the book, but she reported to her roommate that there wasn't a single clipping about Miss Minerva herself.

The furniture in the room, besides the desk, consisted of a single iron bed, a tan wicker armchair, a dark walnut-stained dresser, a cloudy mirror, a straight chair with a leatherette seat. The rug was dark brown. The walls were painted by the college every few years, always the same rather sirupy tan. The floor was stained with a dark reddish-brown oil stain.

Miss Minerva had a bathroom all her own, which was more than some of the younger teachers had. In it there were a tub on claw-end legs, a bowl, a toilet with a brown cracked seat cover, and a small painted cupboard. There was also a dingy radiator which hissed all winter, and on this Miss Minerva kept a flat board to hold supplies.

The water faucet in the tub had been dripping for five years, and someday the college would get around to fixing it. Meanwhile it went on dripping, but she got used to it after a year or two. Even if she had been the executive homemaker type, she couldn't have done anything about it, for outside plumbers were not allowed by the college manager, Mr. Black. Nobody could have anything repaired without his sanction.

Miss Minerva ate all her meals in the dining room of Main Hall, presiding at a table for eight. She said grace before dinner every night. The other faculty members often ate at the Brass Kettle or downtown, or even went away week ends, but she never did. The only change in food she ever experienced during the school year was when the dietition was changed.

She gave her lessons in the basement of Main Hall, where a corridor had been fitted with tiny practice rooms. The piano was almost as old as she was. Through the window came all the steam from the college laundry, with the smell of bleach and soap.

The music department of Buckley was like many music departments in small coeducational colleges or women's colleges. Buckley was a school for "liberal arts," but there was nothing liberal about the curriculum and absolutely no emphasis on arts. This was before the war had been stirred like yeast into the life of the school.

Music and painting were looked upon by the rest of the faculty as light studies. Only mathematics and Latin and Greek and physics and biology really disciplined the mind, they said; they were basic subjects. Psychology

and economics were all right for padding. Spanish was
too easy to do anybody any real good. French was on a
slightly higher level, but not much.

Miss Minerva gave her lessons and put on her student
recitals, therefore, without anybody's bothering. And
this might have gone on forever, except that the college
acquired a new president, and he was a new broom.

The first year he "retired" several secretaries who were
too old to take dictation. The second year, the history
and German departments had a retread. This year, the
third, he was turning his attention to music and art.

"Minnie will get the ax," said Cora Lee.

"It's about time. But she's so tight, she must have a
mint of money," said Jinx, her roommate.

Cora Lee pulled on a lemon-yellow sweater and
stepped into her moccasins. "Well, I got to ankle over
and learn how to sing like Hilda Larsen," she said. "The
recital is day after tomorrow. You coming?"

"I hear your voice too much," said Jinx. "And honestly, those recitals! Do they stink!"

"All I can say is my voice hasn't gone backwards."

"I think you're positively psychotic to keep on with
Minnie all this time," Jinx told her.

"I want the A. It's the easiest way I know to get it."
Cora Lee made herself a deep red mouth. "And don't
forget Minnie's going to get me an audition with Hilda
Larsen if and when I get to New York. She practically
promised."

"Somehow I can't quite feature Minnie the Mouse and
Hilda Larsen," yawned Jinx.

Cora Lee went out. The campus was bright with color,
sweaters in every shade, socks to match. It was exciting

and new to wear short skirts and socks and flat moccasins. Last year, stockings were required, but someway the rule had eased up. The laxness that was to end in jeans and boys' shirts with the tails out was already beginning.

The Wistaria hung a purple veil over the porch of Main, and Cora Lee stopped under it a moment and looked up. It was like being roofed in violet. She hummed a bit of *St. Louis Blues*. Cora Lee had the best voice in Buckley, and the best that Miss Minerva had ever had during all the years. It was resonant, naturally sweet, and climbed easily up to the highest notes. She could sing the *Bell Song* from *Lakme* and keep the notes smooth as honey. The songs Miss Minerva helped her with she did less well, being hampered by the rather odd ideas Minerva had, but the songs she sang without benefit of instruction she sang like an angel.

She was majoring in history.

Cora Lee was a hard, practical-minded girl. She had no patience with softness. She believed in buttering your own bread, and buttering it well. It was not an age of sentiment. She would have said there was not a vulnerable spot in her whole being. She was in love, because that was the thing, but she didn't lie awake at night brooding about it. Maury said she was colder than Little America. And looked like a perfect rose.

As she turned into the practice corridor, she met the violin teacher and nodded briefly to him. His job was safe, even if he couldn't play on key, because his wife was related to the chairman of the board of trustees. But Miss Minnie, she thought, was a dead duck right now.

"Now, we'll just run over your songs for the recital," said Minerva. "I'm not quite satisfied with the last phrase in the *Fairy Pipers*."

"Why can't I sing a new song?" asked Cora Lee perversely.

Miss Minerva looked shocked. "In building a program," she said in her dry, tight voice, "one has to take certain things into consideration."

"Such as what?"

"Balance," said Miss Minerva vaguely, "and—proportion."

Cora Lee opened her lips to say something nasty about never learning anything new, and then shut them again. Miss Minerva looked bad, she noticed. She always looked like a horse, but today her face was gray. She wore a brown dress shaped like a sack, and a pair of old brown shoes. The hem of the dress had partly come down. The shoes were muddy. And the hair net on her rusty hair had a large hole in it, from which a clump of hair stuck out.

"She needs a good currying," thought Cora Lee with disgust.

Miss Minerva spread her large bony hands over the yellowed keys and nodded her head briskly. "Remember the phrasing," she said, and banged out the first chord.

Cora Lee sang. Outside, the laundry boy put down the basket of snowy sheets and leaned against the ivied wall, listening. Three girls on their way to gym stopped too. Cora Lee was pleased, but not excited. She knew she could sing, but she was lazy, and she knew that to be a singer required an awful lot of hard work, even if the faculty at Buckley thought it was a cinch. A career didn't interest her, so she made little effort really to arouse an audience.

Maybe, she thought, looking at Miss Minerva, maybe if she'd an inspiring teacher these four years, she might have gone on—made something of her voice. But she hadn't learned a single thing; she had been bored to death, she was fed up. This was her last recital, and if she knew the signs, Miss Minerva's last one, too. The fairy pipers would quit playing. She laughed at the thought.

Miss Minerva made clucking noises and pushed the pedal sharply. "I think you better sing it again," she said, "and then we'll run over your last number."

When Cora Lee finally left, Miss Minerva sat at the piano, her elbow on the music rack, her head supported by her hand. It was time to wash up and get to the dining room before the herd of students stampeded in. This was fish day. *Bless this food to our use, and us to Thy faithful service.* But she wasn't hungry, she didn't want to eat. A deep thick fear had settled in her bosom under the cotton brassière.

Hilda Larsen was coming to sing at the Opera House. It was the kind of thing that could never happen. As fantastic as the way one could never get on the streetcar to go downtown without finding one's worst enemy on that same streetcar. It was the way deserters always met their chief officer in some bar in a foreign port.

And yet it was going to happen. For the chain of circumstances wasn't really strange. Hilda Larsen's manager was the same one who had arranged for the concert which a great baritone was to give in the Opera House, and a sudden indisposition on the part of the latter made a shift necessary. Hilda Larsen just happened to be on the way to Miami and could stop over one night without upsetting anything. She didn't care, she was always trying to get off trains and stop over. Trains bored her.

The notice appeared in the *Daily Crescent*. Hilda Larsen, world-famous diva, the notice said wildly, would appear in place of the great star. Having dazzled the crowned heads of Europe, what more fitting than that she should come to Buckley and dazzle the subscribers for the concert series so capably managed by Fitzlee Andrews?

Miss Minerva was shivering as she sat at the piano, though the spring air coming in was warm even in the basement. The whole world was in an ecstasy of blossoming and sweet smell and exciting color. But Miss Minerva crept blindly up the stairs without noticing. Her bad knee creaked as she climbed the curlicues to her room and closed the door and sank down on the sagging bed.

When she looked up, she saw the cold, confident eyes of the young girl in the picture looking right at her, and uttering a small broken cry, she buried her face in her hands and wept.

The afternoon of the recital was hot, with the penetrating unseasonal heat of some spring days. The campus lawns were brilliant green, and the Wistaria already was blown, so amethyst petals strewed the steps. But it was cool in the chapel when Miss Minerva came in, blinking at the dimness after dazzle.

They had mimeographed programs, always too many. Nobody ever came to the recitals except the people who were performing or some relative unlucky enough to be visiting at the time. Or a few music students from other teachers. Today there were more than usual because there was a Y.W. meeting right afterward, and the Y.W. people drifted in. And just at the beginning, the heavy metal doors swung open to admit the president and a couple of board members who sat down inconspicuously in the rear.

Cora Lee was standing at the edge of the gray cyclorama, looking out. She wore a plain gray dress and her hair was gold as it fell softly down her neck. She looked scornfully at the audience; it was nothing to her. She was finished with singing anyway. Too much bother. None of this attic stuff for her, she thought contemptuously; she wanted a white satin cover on her bed. She looked over at Miss Minerva, and wondered what was wrong with her. Her eyes were red and the lids puffy. She was a sight. Worse than usual, which was bad enough.

Miss Minerva always wore a beaded crêpe dress in a queer metallic-blue shade. And pointed kid pumps. The dress, she always said, had come from Paris. "Well, about the time Paris was founded," Cora Lee said to herself. Years when dresses were short, Minerva trotted over to the little dressmaker and had the hem taken up; other years she had it let down. The former hemlines were visible when long skirts were in. And now the dress had an unfortunate way of shedding beads, so Minerva walked with the faint, tinkly sound of falling glass.

Miss Minerva accompanied her students, striking the keynote separately before each chord, and if there seemed to be any doubt about it, striking it several times. And every time the student hit a high note, Minerva turned her face sharply and faced the audience as if to say, "You see, she really got there!" Even the way she turned her head looked horselike, and her pawing at the pedals emphasized the effect. She came down on the pedals at random, but with vigor.

Cora Lee, waiting her turn, saw the president shifting

restlessly in his seat. He whispered something to the man beside him, who nodded. Cora Lee had no doubt about their reason for being at the recital. And it would be a good thing to fire Miss Minnie, the poor old horse.

A weak spattering of hands marked the end of *I Hear a Thrush at Eve*, sung doubtfully by Mary Jane Winter.

Cora Lee went out and stood waiting for her chord. Now she could see how dreadfully pale Miss Minerva looked; her whole face had a greenish look, except that under her eyes were smears of purple.

Miss Minerva gave her a ghastly imitation of a smile and brought her hands down on the keys. Her hands were trembling.

"She knows," thought Cora Lee. She looked at her teacher's anxious eyes and suddenly, for no reason at all, felt a twinge of sympathy. This was too much like cornering a rabbit and closing in for the kill. Minnie might not know anything, but she worked all the time there was. She never did anything else but work. Never went anywhere, never had any fun, never saw anybody but the students. Cora Lee thought, "Oh, to blazes with it, I'll show 'em she's got a good one."

And she really put her mind, for once, on her singing. After her first number there was a stir of attention. The second, which of course was *Ave Maria*, made even more of an impression. The clapping was genuine and enthusiastic. And a faint color came into Miss Minerva's gray cheeks.

Cora Lee did the *Fairy Pipers*, a song she detested thoroughly. She could just imagine chasing around after fairy pipers, and the thing was so old it was falling apart at the seams. But today she sang it as if she enjoyed it.

> "When all the birds have gone to sleep
> And all the frogs are still. . . ."

She had them all intent, and it felt good and it was easy. She let the notes come out pure and round.

> "Airy fairy pipers underneath the silver moon. . . ."

And when the program was over, Miss Minerva was taking her hand, quite speechless. Cora Lee got away as fast as she could. She didn't like the strange sensation of pity which had been with her on the stage. What in time was the matter with her, getting all soft and silly? She'd cut the next lesson. Her mark was safe after today.

As she went to the mailbox to see if she had the daily letter from Maury, she saw the poster on the bulletin board.

"Oh, Cora Lee, this means you!" called her roommate, and she stopped to see what she meant.

A special block of seats for the Hilda Larsen concert was being reserved for the college. And the morning before, Hilda Larsen was going to give auditions to the three best students in the music department.

"So that's Jones and Bender and you," said Jinx. "And look, if you get a scholarship at Juilliard, how about me coming up to live with you?"

"Nonsense," said Cora Lee. "I'm not bothering."

"Don't you even want to meet Hilda Larsen?"

"What for?"

"Well, think of seeing the ideal after hearing about her all this time from Minnie. Say—do you suppose she'll come out and eat at our table? We'll have a lion in our dining room!"

The babble increased. Everybody began to speculate now about Hilda and Miss Minerva. Curious and eager as kittens, they wondered whether they could go down to the train in a gang and watch the meeting. Was Minnie going to wear that old brown suit? And the shoes? And the hat with the dead finch on it?

Inside of half an hour the whole corridor was echoing with excited voices. A real celebrity! And their own obscure voice teacher! Why, it was really romantic! Probably Hilda Larsen would be there for Sunday dinner, in which case certainly they would have turkey and cranberry sauce and ice cream, even if it were not Thanksgiving. They had turkey for John Mason Brown, and he couldn't sing; he just talked.

Cora Lee had lab that next afternoon. On her way down the long corridor, she passed the president's office and looked in to nod and speak. He made a point of keeping his door open so the students would feel that he was really part of the group. The result was that many of them scurried past because they couldn't think of anything to murmur as he looked up from his desk.

Today as Cora Lee glanced in, she saw that he had a visitor in the chair by the desk. Miss Minerva Martin was sitting there; there was no mistaking her narrow stiff back, and she had the black-and-white print on too. As Cora Lee looked, the president's secretary stepped quietly across the room and closed the door.

"Well," thought Cora Lee, "he's giving her the gate early. Good riddance for Buckley." She shook her head scornfully and went on up to the lab. There was no reason for her to give it another thought, and yet she did. Possibly it was because twice a week for four years she

had spend half an hour with Miss Minerva. Maybe even
if you despised a person, that much time with her made
some kind of link.

Cora Lee couldn't explain it, but she felt restless all
during lab, even more restless than usual. Miss Minnie
must have plenty of money after all these years of spending absolutely nothing. And even if she got the sack, she
would have all the glory of Hilda Larsen's appearance.
Think of how jealous the rest of the music department
would be! Not one of them knew a single celebrity.
Why, it was a triumph. After all the years of her talking
and bragging about Hilda Larsen, now she had a chance
to bring her right out on campus. Imagine the great Larsen sitting up in the awful room facing the picture of
herself as a young girl. Imagine her at the table while
Miss Minnie bent her long face and said, "Bless this food
to our use, and us to Thy faithful service!"

Cora Lee, as soon as lab was over, started to her room
along the bridgeway. Well, maybe she better let Minnie
know she was not coming to lesson tomorrow. Kind of
mean to let her sit and wait there all period in that old
cellar room.

"I ought to have my head examined," thought Cora
Lee. "What do I care for? I'll tell her I'm quitting. For
good. Just a rat leaving the sinking ship."

She climbed the curlicues, went down the dark hall,
and tapped at Miss Minerva's door. There was a little
silence and then a murmur and Cora Lee went in.

Miss Minerva was sitting at the desk, with a little pile
of underwear and towels beside her.

She gave Cora Lee a vague look and said in a low voice,
"I am making out my laundry list."

"I don't mean to bother you," said Cora Lee, feeling uneasy.

"Not at all, not at all," murmured Minerva. "I just thought it was best to list the laundry. One doesn't like to make trouble for people. Does one?"

"No, no, I guess not."

Cora Lee gave her message, but she only said she couldn't come the next day. Someway she didn't feel so ruthless. There was something about Miss Minnie. . . .

"I won't be here either," said Miss Minerva.

Cora Lee went along the hall again. She had something niggling around the back of her mind. Minnie looked—queer. "One doesn't like to make trouble"; what did she mean by that? Nobody else would list her laundry for her, in any case. Either she sent it to the college plant or she didn't. Whom would she be saving trouble for? Where was she going?

Cora Lee got to her room, and slipped off her sweater and began to brush her shining fall of hair. Her face stared back at her, but she wasn't thinking about how beautiful she was. She was puzzling about that laundry list.

Was Minnie touched in the head after that talk with the president? The only reason there would be for anybody else to make out her laundry list would be that she was in the infirmary.

"Or dead," thought Cora Lee suddenly. She laid down the hairbrush and stared at her image in the glass and saw that she was turning white. "But how silly; I must have read too many whodunits," she thought. "Certainly there isn't—there can't be. . . . Why, Hilda Larsen will be here tonight! On the five-forty-five. This is her hour in the sun!"

But Cora Lee pulled her sweater on again and started running back along the corridor. "I am just going to speak to her again," she thought, apologizing to herself.

She didn't even knock; she opened the door and peeked in, making no sound. Miss Minerva was silhouetted against the rectangle of window that the devouring ivy had spared, and she held a bottle in her hand.

"Miss Martin," said Cora Lee, "may I come in?" and she moved inside the room quickly.

Miss Minerva gave a start and looked blankly at Cora Lee. Then a deep dark flush spread slowly over the paleness of her face. She stammered, "I—have a headache—pill. . . ."

But Cora Lee went to her and firmly took the bottle. "I wouldn't take a pill right now," she said. "You come down to the drugstore with me for some hot tea!"

And then, hearing the kindness in her voice, they were both astounded. And either the strangeness of it, or the fact that Miss Minerva was really at the end of her rope, made her suddenly collapse on the bed and cover her face with her hands in the age-old gesture of a woman stricken.

"Oh dear, oh dear, oh dear," she said monotonously.

"Miss Minerva, you mustn't feel bad," Cora Lee said. "It really isn't so bad as all that."

"Bad?" asked Minerva. "Yes, it couldn't be any worse."

There was a finality about the words. After she had said them, she pushed her straggling hair back and lifted her head and sat very quietly, staring at Cora Lee and yet not focusing her eyes on her.

Cora Lee didn't know what to do. Her natural instinct

was always to avoid unpleasant scenes by going away from them as fast as possible. But now she had a compelling sense that she must not, simply must not leave Miss Minerva, not until she felt better. She cast about in her mind for the right words of comfort.

"Hilda Larsen will be here tonight," she said. "And you'll want to see her and have a nice long visit. . . ."

"Hilda Larsen," said Miss Minerva, "has never seen me in her life!"

The effect of this staggering piece of news was to confuse Cora Lee completely. "Why, you can't say that!" she said. "There's her picture right there on your wall!"

"I bought it," said Miss Minerva, "from the photo shop in Snowshoe, Minnesota, when I was at home years and years ago."

"Bought it?"

"Yes," Miss Minerva told her. "For a dollar and forty cents."

Cora Lee sat down on the desk chair. But if Minerva had bought that picture, then Hilda Larsen had never given it to her—and then if she hadn't . . . well, then, she did not owe her career to having taken lessons of Minerva. And all that story of Minerva's was a plain lie.

"I made it all up," said Miss Minerva, confirming her discovery.

"But—but whatever for?" Cora Lee asked.

"I didn't have anything," explained Minerva, pinching up little pieces of her dress. "I just didn't."

"But what good did it do to pretend about her?"

"It gave me something to be proud of," said Miss Minerva. "Everybody has to have one thing in the world to be proud of. So I had Hilda Larsen."

In the silence that fell, the sound of the voice on the

campus came like the twitter of gathering swallows at twilight. The late sun laid a level wash of gold against the dusty pane and the air was unbearably sweet as it stirred the brown lace curtains. It was just too beautiful a world, too full of riches.

"I didn't mind not teaching any more," said Minerva. "I knew that would come. But having it come right this week, right when she is coming . . . you can see how it is, Cora Lee."

"Yes, I see."

"But you run along now, it's nearly time for dinner," said Minerva. "I'll just tidy up a bit and come down in time to say the blessing. I don't want to make any trouble for anybody."

"Heavens on earth," thought Cora, "does she mean she won't take too many of those pills? Or that she will wait until she's presided at the table so the dining room won't be upset now that it's so near dinnertime? Why can't a person ever understand what's going on inside someone?"

And this was the first time in her life Cora Lee had ever wanted to understand what was going on inside anybody except herself.

"What would you do if you didn't come back?" she asked.

"I have a little house out at the edge of Snowshoe," said Miss Minerva. "My sister has always lived there; that is, until she died."

"I didn't know you had a sister," Cora Lee said.

"She'd always been delicate—" Minerva spoke slowly, "and as long as I had to take care of her, I really don't know what would have happened if I had lost my position. I really don't."

"You mean you have been supporting her all the time?"

"She was delicate, she had to rest a good deal," Miss Minerva explained. "But she died last summer."

"Oh, dear," said Cora Lee.

"One can manage on very little," said Minerva; "really very little. It takes more for two. Much more."

Out of the chaos in her mind, Cora Lee found an idea. "I will run along," she said, just as if they had been having tea. "But I really came to tell you I want to sing for Hilda Larsen in the morning and I want you to promise you will go over the music with me before I go. Will you?"

Miss Minerva stopped pinching the silk. "Why, yes, Cora Lee," she said, "I will. I would really be a bad woman if I didn't, wouldn't I? And as they always say, the play's the thing, my dear, the play's the thing."

Cora Lee hurried along the shadowy walk, and got the college taxi. "I want to meet the five-forty-five," she said, "and you'll just have to step on it."

"I can't make it," he said. "It's five-twenty now."

"Make it anyhow," said Cora Lee.

She braced her moccasins against the rail and clung to the seat as they swayed and jolted along the back streets. And she kept going over the whole thing again.

Miss Minerva hadn't been a miser, she didn't have any money. She had scrimped and pinched and lived like nothing on earth and never once peeped about it. Every other faculty member who had cousins to help through school or sick mothers or anything just went to town about it. But Miss Minerva said nothing. She's worn those awful clothes without a murmur, never wangled an invitation to dinner, never toadied to anybody. They had laughed at her, taken her off in skits year after year, the young and fortunate. And now she was pushed out on the plank to sink or swim, and nobody would even notice it. They'd never give her a banquet, and a gold watch.

What made it all the worse was that you couldn't figure what she had to make life worth living. Because the gifted, the exciting, the successful teachers always had that relationship with the students. Like Cora Lee had with Doctor Palmer, the Shakespeare man. Lots of the teachers had their pets, their little circle, and maybe they got warmth enough out of that. But Cora Lee, the best Minerva ever had or could hope to have, had barely been civil to her. Arrogant, hard, rude, scornful. All these words came to Cora Lee now. Lazy, too.

They heard the whistle of the train as it slowed for the junction. "Might yet make it," said the driver, getting interested himself in the race.

So Minerva's life had been built around the myth of Hilda Larsen. And now that was over too. What a scandal it would make. The campus would boil with it like a teakettle over the hottest fire. Cora Lee knew herself and her fellow students very well. They would giggle, and make remarks, and point out, and ask demure questions to turn the knife. The laughingstock of the college. Defenseless.

It was horrible to think of, it was a humiliation nobody could endure. The faculty members would not be above joining in. "People don't like to feel tricked," thought Cora Lee. No, if it got out in the morning that Hilda Larsen said she never had heard of Miss Minerva Martin, every last thing would fall down on the poor old thing.

"Here she comes," said the driver.

"I'll pay you tomorrow," said Cora Lee. "Meet me in front of Main at nine-thirty. I want to go downtown anyhow. 'By now."

She slammed the door and ran down the platform as the train stopped and the porters swung down the steep steps. Her hair was flying, and her sweater was smudged from the lab. For once, she had no time to make herself a mouth.

She ran down to the Pullmans and got to the last car just as Hilda Larsen stepped out, elegant in gray and blue, and followed respectfully by her accompanist and three pigskin bags.

"Miss Larsen," said Cora Lee, "I do not want an autograph."

Hilda Larsen's ice-blue eyes looked surprised.

"I want to ride to the hotel and have an interview," said Cora Lee, "before you see anybody else."

Miss Larsen was bored. She looked at Cora Lee. She was also a hard woman, and maybe she recognized some quality in Cora Lee's face that reminded her of herself at that age—heaven knew how long ago.

"Okay, baby," she said. "I'll hear your story." She turned on the sweating accompanist. "Don't scratch those bags, Ivan."

If Cora Lee had been timid, or soft, or adoring, or almost anything she should have been, the story would have ended before they got to the Carroll Hotel. But Cora Lee was not afraid of anything, and she was hard and sure and she ignored the fact that Hilda Larsen was a great singer, a fabulously successful woman, a second or third Jenny Lind. She just sat there and told the truth, while the heady scent of Hilda's million-dollar perfume filled the musty old taxi. She talked about Snowshoe, and Hilda remembered her dreary, mean youth. And she talked about this woman who made her whole life out of a dream of just knowing Hilda.

And all Hilda said when they reached the hotel was, "Bring her with you tomorrow. I'll hear you sing. I suppose you sing like a crow."

"You'll be surprised," said Cora Lee.

The whole college blazed with excitement. Everything else was forgotten. The girls in Main wore a special smug look. For it was in their dining room that Hilda Larsen sat, right at Minerva's table, looking just out of this world and laughing and talking. Her diamonds caught the light and flashed. Her perfume was sniffed by a hundred eager young noses. Miss Minerva looked dazed. Cora Lee sat on the other side of Miss Larsen, eating her broccoli silently, but smiling a funny little smile.

The president sat between Hilda Larsen and Miss Minerva. He was planning a farewell banquet and had made discreet inquiries as to whether Miss Minerva had a gold watch or not. After all, Buckley should recognize an old, faithful teacher who was responsible for the beginning of a singer like Hilda Larsen. It gave tone to the place.

Hilda Larsen drank tea laced with honey and explained she would have a sandwich later on. She declined the banquet but was very regretful, she said. She must be on the Flyer the next noon, but would listen to prospective singers at ten.

It was noon when Cora Lee and Hilda Larsen and Miss Minerva came from the auditorium. Miss Minerva blinked in the harsh light. Cora Lee was pale but composed. Hilda Larsen looked down the leafy drive for her taxi.

"You can sing," she spoke abruptly to Cora Lee. "What are you going to do about it? A voice is just a beginning."

Cora Lee didn't answer. Miss Minerva had a dreamy ecstatic look and hardly listened. None of this she would ever understand. How could Hilda Larsen remember hearing her sing in the Methodist church, decide to look up her old friend, and actually say she done a wonderful job with young singers like Cora Lee?

"It shows how wrong one is to despair," she thought humbly, "for one never knows. Around the corner it may be different."

And she trotted stiffly along, happier than any angel in Heaven.

"And I am responsible for Cora Lee going on with her career," she thought, and that was the ultimate fulfillment any teacher could desire.

Strangely enough, Miss Minerva was right. For certainly the fact that Cora Lee went on to be called the fourth Jenny Lind was indeed due to her, though not in the way she thought.

Portrait
of a Gentleman

✸✸✸✸✸✸✸✸✸✸✸✸   ✸

Tim moved down the street, lifting his paws delicately. He held his head high; the plume of his tail streamed straight behind him as befitted a gentleman Irish setter. It was morning; he had his rounds to make.

The sun felt warm on his thick dark-red curls; he swung his ears; sniffed the fresh smells. Behind him, at a respectful distance, followed Jennifer. When he stopped, Jennifer checked her fat little body; when he went on, she went too. She was only a puppy.

Tim's first stop was the old brown house around the corner. He barked at the back door. Mrs. Weissmuller came out, wiping her face with a towel. "Ja, you Tim," she rumbled. "No meat today yet. Vait a minute."

She brought a doughnut. Tim slanted an eye at it, thumped his tail slightly. Jennifer sat down, her tongue lolloping out.

"Poor Tim," sighed Mrs. Weissmuller, "what are you going to do? . . ."

Tim went sedately down the steps, the doughnut in his mouth. As soon as he was out of sight, he dropped it. Jennifer fell on it, making disgusting puppy noises.

Suddenly Tim stopped, lifted his left paw, stood still as stone, pointing. Only his nose wrinkled with excitement. Then he skimmed across the yard smooth as a shot. The white chicken squawked, then ran wildly. Tim stopped and barked happily. The chicken kept on running.

Absorbed in watching, Tim failed to notice Miss Connie until he was close enough to catch the sweet scent that came with her. Miss Connie was his second-best friend. He wagged his whole body. Miss Connie gave a faint scream.

"Oh, Timothy—are you at it again?"

He wagged harder.

"Timothy Pepper, that's one of the Jones' prize hens! Whatever will Dick say?" She came up and eyed him sternly. He drooped his plume and looked innocent. "You've got to stop scaring chickens because you'll only get in a jam."

Tim stiffened, made a protesting rumble. Connie stood over him. "Run home fast," she said. "I'll see what I can do, in case old man Jones saw you."

Sadly Tim loitered on, his head cocked. Jennifer rose and followed. When she came too near, Tim made threatening noises in his throat.

Suddenly he whipped his nose high. He was off again. Louisa the cat lay basking on the walk, large and yellow.

He liked her, but he liked to tease. He made a bound at her and barked loudly.

Louisa saw him and rushed for the porch with a shrill scream. Dodging an ice wagon, Tim leaped after her. There was a lovely chase, under the porch, across a flower bed, through a clothesline of wet clothes, ending finally at Louisa's back door. Then Tim checked his wild rush, circled around barking loudly. He affected an interest in a hoptoad under the rhubarb leaves. He became magnificently indifferent. Then at a safe distance he gave tongue again, telling Louisa what he would do the next time he saw her.

He went on. He had the funny feeling in his stomach that meant it was time to be getting home to the adorable one, and Dick. So he took a short cut. He let his legs out and really ran, leaving Jennifer panting far in the rear. For several blocks, he raced a passing automobile, his ears flapping, tail waving with sheer joy. Now and then he gave a joyous bark.

He considered the matter of rabbits. It was worth a few minutes. He swerved and made for a large vegetable garden. A brown shadow scuttled away from the lettuce patch. Quivering with ecstasy, Tim pursued. He dove through the neat rows of vegetables. The rabbit humped rapidly ahead, finally whisked under the side of the house. Tim made a head dive and brought up under the house, halfway in.

He found the hole pretty small. He squeezed and wedged. He scrabbled with his paws. But he couldn't make it. Painfully he shoved himself backward only to discover he was stuck fast. He worked desperately; his hind legs were safe outside but his body was pinned tight. He panted. He made his stomach small. It wasn't possible that he couldn't get out. He had got in. This was puzzling.

After a long time, he gave up and rested his bruised paws. He whined his troubled whine. That always brought the adorable one. She came whenever he called her. The loveliest blue eyes in the world always saw instantly when he had burrs in his tail or wanted a drink. Her hands rubbed the hurt places so softly, and the sweet flower smell of her . . . he closed his eyes and cried like a very young puppy. His back was being broken. He could hardly breathe.

"I declare, there's Dick and Jinny's dog!" He heard a voice from outside. Other voices came booming in. He stretched his weary neck and rolled an anguished eye.

There were scratching noises. He saw the damp earth being moved out. It seemed to disappear by a magic process on a large flat thing. Moving with difficulty, he scratched with his forepaws and helped move the dirt. The opening slowly grew larger. He squirmed. Somebody laid hold of the rear end of his body and tugged. With a flurry of dirt, he came out and felt the cool air on his nose again.

"Poor Tim," said the man. "He'll be lost now without. . . ."

It was high time he got home. He felt better. He loped away.

It had rained the night before. There was a lovely puddle where the road curved. He rolled in it, splashing the muddy water all over his shining coppery fur. This was taboo, but it was lovely. He rolled luxuriously. As he swept the water over him, he saw his third-best friend wheeling a baby carriage down the street.

He rose and joyously made his way to her, dripping

mud and water. As he approached, he shook vigorously. Then he leaped on her, planting muddy paws on her dress. A wet tongue lapped her pleasantly. She took him walking very often when she wheeled the fat baby in the carriage.

"Oh, Tim—look what you're doing!" She retreated. "Tim—get away!"

She slapped him. He sat down abruptly on his haunches. She turned her back on him. His ears dropped. His tail sagged. She wasn't glad to see him. His eyes stared at her, wondering. She wasn't glad to see him.

He went on, sniffing the air. There was a funny smell across the way. A lot of men stood around a funny machine breathing smoke and fire. The roadway was black and shining. A strong scent came from it, a different scent. It looked wet. He put his paws on it. When he lifted them, they were covered with black sticky stuff. He backed out and started again. Then he lifted a paw and licked it. The stuff was thick and bad on his tongue. One of the men saw him and shouted. A stone whizzed past his ears. He ran, dodged, clipped out of sight behind a hedge. His paws were black.

It was time to hurry to the adorable one. A nice dish of fresh steak and oatmeal, a nap, and a walk with Dick and the adorable one. That would be fine.

He cut a corner. A boy stopped to pat him. There was something in the boy's hand wrapped in paper. It smelled like—it was raw meat. Tim, indifferent, lounged after the boy. The boy went up the steps of a strange house and laid the package on the back porch.

When the boy went away, Tim padded up the steps and took the bundle carefully in his mouth. He lifted his head proudly, waved his tail, skimmed away. This was a real find.

He ran faster as he neared home. He had the funny home feeling in his stomach again. He couldn't wait.

Every day, after his morning round, he had dinner and a nap and then Dick said, "How about a walk, old man?" and then he sat up straight, holding his paw in the air until the adorable one laughed and said, "All right, let's get started." That was a real walk, in the woods. Squirrels, birds, rushes and barkings, and the two coming behind.

He always had to wait for them. Run back and bark it out in the ears of the adorable one. Turn with paw lifted and look over his shoulder until she called, "Go on, dear." Then flash away, up and down and back, to wait for her again. She came behind, very slowly, leaning on a stick.

He ran. He whipped up the walk, barked happily at the door. Nobody came. He raised a paw and scratched the door. When at last someone came, it was a stranger. He bounded in, dragging the bundle of meat. "Woof!" he announced loudly, "Woof, woof, woof!"

"Hush," said the woman who let him in.

There was a strange smell in the house. Garden smell, but close and hot. He ran to the kitchen and found his water dish bone dry. Two girls were standing there. He asked for a drink. They ignored him, so he asked again, speaking louder. There was nothing for it but his best trick. His mouth was hot. He sat up straight, his forepaws hanging folded in front. It was frightfully hard to balance. He swayed slightly, kept himself up with difficulty, wrinkled his forehead.

"Look at the dog!" one girl said, "he wants something."

"He's doing a trick."

Even then they did nothing. Humans could be stupid. He went to the water dish and sniffed. He barked.

"Maybe he wants a drink."

He drank then, picked up his bundle and hurried upstairs. Most of the paper was gone now and red meat stuck out. His mouth watered, but he held the meat without tearing.

At the door of her room he stopped suddenly. For as his paws crossed the sill, he knew she wasn't there. The last time he had looked for her, she hadn't been there. Dimly he was conscious of looking for her a number of times. He laid the meat carefully on the carpet and padded to the bed. The flower scent of the adorable one was gone. There was a sleepy odor instead, odor belonging to men carrying black bags, and he backed away from it, his skin prickling.

His play slipper lay on the floor. He nosed it, flopped it over absently with a paw. He barked anxiously. He wanted her. He looked for her in the closet. He looked behind the bureau, under the table. Then he made a hurried tour of the whole upstairs. It was empty.

Returning, he stretched his body across the doorway, his head on his paws, his brow wrinkled. His stomach was full of the funny hurt. Motionless, he waited. Half drearily, he snapped at a fly. The sun was going down. After a while it went away altogether.

When it was quite dark, Tim went downstairs to the kitchen. He looked at his supper, but quickly turned and left it. He couldn't eat. He heard noises outside the house.

Standing on his hind legs, he pressed his cold nose against the glass and looked out. There was the puppy Jennifer yapping at a squirrel.

Tim got down and once more went upstairs. The room was still empty. He went then to the closed door of Dick's room. It was taboo to disturb Dick when he was working. Tim sat by the closed door, rubbed his nose against the knob. Moving inch by inch, he edged his body closer, pushing harder and harder.

The door swung open and he crouched flat, waiting for punishment. Then he cocked his head in surprise. Dick was in the far corner in the big chair but he didn't notice the sound. He was so still Tim thought he must be asleep, but when Tim stole nearer, paw by paw, he saw Dick's eyes wide open and fixed.

The red plume beat the floor. Tim sat as close as he dared. After a while he thudded his tail harder. Then delicately he laid his muzzle on Dick's knee and rested his cold nose against the hand nearest. He kept his eyes on Dick's face.

Dick started slightly and looked down. There was a long pause, neither of them moving a muscle. Then, very slowly, Dick's hand buried itself in the soft silky place behind the dog's ears. "Hello—old man," he said in a queer voice.

Tim pressed his head against Dick's arm.

"Guess we'll have to look out for each other," said Dick huskily. He reached for his hat and got up slowly.

They left the dark house together.

The Legend of Lavinia

✿✿✿✿✿✿✿✿✿✿✿✿   ✿

They had lived together for years in the little sturdy house at the end of Maple Street. The house was built by Ella May Mott's great-grandfather, and built for time. Ella May herself was born there and after she graduated from high school she lived there with her mother. Once in those early days, a man from West Bend, Indiana, came to town briefly to work on the Cherry Street Bridge and he fell in love with Ella May, but of course Ella May couldn't leave her mother alone in the house and go off. Her mother had crippling arthritis and it was out of the question.

When her mother died, Lavinia Brewster moved in with Ella May. Lavinia was the librarian in the old red-brick library. She was slender and really lovely looking in a dark quiet way. She had shining dark eyes and dark soft hair firmly restrained under the heavy hair net. Ella

May's pale blue-eyed prettiness made a pleasant contrast as they walked home in the late afternoon in their neat flower-print dresses, well-polished ground grippers, and white cotton lace gloves.

They had a lovely life. The little house, smelling faintly of lavender, was cool and tranquil in the hot summer and warmed with a sufficiency of shiny fat stoves in winter. Ella May had a fine garden and on Saturday afternoons in summer she put on her wide straw hat and firm garden gloves and worked happily with the roses and the delphinium and the amaryllis. There was a great Calycanthus bush by the front door. Lavinia restricted her gardening to pinching the dark velvety blooms and sniffing the spicy, rich, musky scent they gave. But Ella May was a weeder and a waterer and a mulcher. And a pruner. No straggling branches, no ragged rose shoots in her garden; it was neat as a freshly ironed damask.

In the little valley town, Lavinia and Ella May were as sound and solid as the columns of the bank where Ella May worked carefully and faithfully and precisely. She never made a mistake.

She was a person of whom you might say she never did make a mistake.

But she made one!

Tea was a special event at the Mott house. On sizzling August afternoons, Lavinia and Ella May made fresh pots of Orange Pekoe and Lavinia added various fruit juices and they called it Russian tea although it was no more Russian than apple pan dowdy. It was a little spicy, a little too sweet, and they were proud of it. Ella May made paper-thin bread-and-butter slices and Lavinia did the little sponge squares on alternate Saturdays.

For they shared everything. They divided the chores, they never bickered; one week it was Ella May's turn to cook; another, it was Lavinia's. When it came to the fall housecleaning, one did the prying up of the carpet tacks and supervising of Jimmy Green, who beat the carpets thoroughly half a day. The other did the polishing of the windows with vinegar and water and soft cheese-cloth.

Lavinia brought home the best books from the library and they read them aloud, one reading, one knitting bootees for the next neighborhood baby. They put little knitted posies on the bootees at the end of the ties, and the booties were exquisite.

They were always available, moreover, for helping at church suppers, or packing baskets for the poor. They were not selfish, they were generous and gentle in all they did.

They loved each other and as the years fell quietly on them, the only change noticeable was that they quoted each other more often. Lavinia said to me last Wednesday ... Ella May feels ... but nobody minded that at all.

Possibly Ella May was more forceful. She decided to paint the house pale yellow instead of white. She changed icemen when too much debris melted with the great chunks of river ice. She decided which nights they would go to the Chatauqua and how much they would contribute to the India Missionary Fund. But Lavinia always smiled and agreed quickly. When Ella May suggested that the lavender print was too old, Lavinia gave it up, although she nourished a passion for lavender. It reminded her of violets by a mossy stone, she said.

But you are not a mossy stone, said Ella May firmly.

Nobody ever knew the date when the exchange minister, Reverend Mr. Sinclair, first met Lavinia. Probably he stopped in the library to borrow a book and walked across the waxy brown floor quietly to the desk where a pale light fell on Lavinia's bent head. Or he might have met her at Peabody's drugstore as she bought a bar of pure castile soap for Ella May's delicate skin. Peabody knew everybody, he could easily have said, I want you to meet our new Preacher—a Presbyterian and a Methodist ought to get together, ha, ha.

Or he might have seen her first at the Chatauqua in the shadowy brown tent that creaked on its stays like an elderly woman in a steel corset. Someone would say, let me introduce. . . .

In any case, in a small town, everybody meets everybody in the end. However, if it hadn't been just when it was. . . .

In any case, the Reverend did a mort of reading. He was always at the library and he always needed help. In muted tones, smiling just a little, Lavinia would advise him. Or go ahead into the stacks, walking lightly as a willow branch. Often she smiled, and her shining eyes picked up every bit of light in the gloomy old pile and gave it back.

When Lavinia suggested gently that they might ask him to tea, the poor man had lost his wife only a year ago and he was a stranger sojourning in a strange land, she said, Ella May was a little tart.

"He's not OUR preacher," said she. "Let the Presbyterians entertain him."

But she thought better of it, and asked him herself when he came into the bank to get a ten-dollar check cashed for his week's living. Something about the way he thanked her so warmly—so. . . .

He sat easily in the little parlor sipping the sweet tea and devouring four slices of the bread and butter and adding sweet-cherry preserve with a will. Against the high back of the rose-velvet chair, his tawny head really seemed luminous and his gray steady eyes were very bright. He discoursed gravely on the subject of man's duty to God, but he also told several rather amusing anecdotes that made the two gentlewomen blush and smile. He was so gay for a minister!

"He seems just like anybody," Ella May summed it up as they rinsed the tea dishes, then washed them, then rinsed them again, then dried them with a warm tea towel.

"He admired your garden," observed Lavinia with a smile.

Ella May was pleased. "Sometime we shall have him for a really good chicken dinner," she said. "I doubt he ever has anything fit to eat at the Fitch's boarding house. That woman. . . ."

"She waters the gravy," said Lavinia in a hushed voice.

Several times after that, the Reverend Mr. Sinclair just happened to be passing as Lavinia and Ella May turned the corner of Vine Street and started down Maple. He escorted them, lifted his hat in farewell. Both of them would look after him, both smiling.

Asking him for dinner, however, presented problems. Two single women could hardly invite a widower, even a minister. It was Ella May who solved it: they gave a small dinner for half a dozen, and invited both ministers. They were very merry as Lavinia made her whipped potatoes and Ella May set the big round oak table with the best sprigged dishes. When the Reverend Mr. Sinclair arrived, he had two boxes of chocolates under his arm, one tied with gauzy blue ribbon, one with red. He gave the blue to Lavinia, the red to Ella May.

"I don't think I ever knew a nicer gentleman," confided Ella May after the party was over. "He reminds me of my father."

Lavinia didn't say anything; she looked tired. Her cheeks were a little flushed under the dusting of rice powder.

"Are you catching a cold?" asked Ella May sharply.

"No, indeed, I am not," said Lavinia. "It's just the party—all the people. . . ." She went upstairs almost immediately and wandered a little aimlessly around her room. She took the ribbon from the candy box and folded it gently and laid it in the drawer.

For the fact was that during the course of charades, the Reverend Mr. Sinclair had spoken an aside to Lavinia, and what he said was, "Do you know, blue is my favorite color?"

Most things move slowly in a little town. The seasons change almost imperceptibly. Who can say just when the first scarlet blazes on the maple, or the cardinal flower burns her glory in the roadside by the old watch factory? Life is ordered, Sunday is for church, Monday is for cleaning and washing, Tuesday is for ironing. Wednesday the Clio Club meets and Thursday is prayer meeting. Friday the baking for the week end makes the day busy. Saturday the farmers come to town; the stores are jammed. The farm horses stand patiently along the curbing, nuzzling their feed bags. In summer, they wear straw hats with holes cut through for their ears.

But now and then the rhythm of the heart makes its own time, and it wasn't more than two weeks after the dinner party that the Reverend Mr. Sinclair came up the steps of the Mott house at seven-thirty in the evening. It was the night Ella May had her D.A.R. meeting. She carried the flag tucked under her arm in a respectful way and she turned to say to Lavinia, "I may be late; we have a committee meeting after." She added, "Set the beans to soak."

Lavinia set the beans to soak. It was frightfully warm, so she took off her dark blue dress and slipped into an old soft cotton with short sleeves and an almost daring neck. When she heard the door knocker sound its solemn brass warning, she picked up the milk bill and went to answer.

But it wasn't the milkman, it was Reverend Mr. Sinclair, a little breathless as if he had been running, except a minister does not run on Maple Street.

Lavinia drew back and her face was a little pale suddenly. "I am sorry," she said, "Miss Mott is out; this is her night at D.A.R."

The Reverend Mr. Sinclair smiled. "I know," he said.

Lavinia had to open the screen door, and he came in and laid his hat on the hall table. She made a gesture toward the parlor and they went in and he sat on the sofa, leaning a little forward and looking at her earnestly. The extraordinary brightness of his eyes contrasted sharply with the pallor of his face.

"Miss Brewster," he began, "I have something to say

to you which I wished to say without Miss Mott being present. Do I make myself clear?"

"Yes," said Lavinia faintly.

"It is not that I am a secretive, nor an underhanded man," he went on firmly, "but there are times when only one person should hear what is said. This is one of them. Will you marry me, Miss Brewster? Will you marry me, Lavinia?"

Her dark eyes widened and she looked at him with shock. The color ebbed from her face until it looked transparent as fine porcelain. Her lips moved, but for a little while no sound came from them.

He said, "I did not mean to unduly advance my cause, but I cannot find it in my heart to delay when I shall so soon be gone. And I—I love you."

For a moment a look of ecstasy came over Lavinia's face. Her dark eyes were brilliant, her mouth soft, and the color was like May wine in her cheeks. One hand lifted toward him with an open palm, and she leaned forward in the Victorian armchair. The pale cotton lace at her throat shivered suddenly with her breathing.

Then she let her hand fall, and closed the slender fingers against the palm.

"While I cannot offer you riches," he was saying in an eager voice, "I can offer you the best that is in me. With God's grace, I should manage to make you comfortable and—and you would be always cherished."

Still Lavinia said nothing. Only a small choking sigh came from her.

In the silence, the sound of the cicadas was loud and brassy in the trees outside.

The Reverend Mr. Sinclair kept his eyes on Lavinia

and when he spoke, his voice was rough. "Am I to understand you cannot—cannot care for me? I had hoped
. . . I felt. . . ."

Lavinia's head was bent. "I care," she whispered.

"Well then, that settles everything," he said joyously.

She lifted her head and looked at him, her face glim-
mering in the shadowy room. "No," she said. "No, I
am afraid not."

"You don't surely mean. . . ."

"Yes," she said.

He flung his tawny head up and the eyes that were
so impressive as he spoke God's word on Sunday from
the golden-oak pulpit were even more impressive now.

"You mean that you will not leave Miss Mott? Lavinia, marriage is a sacrament, ordained by God—for
marriage one leaves Father and Mother and cleaves only
to one. . . ."

Lavinia seemed to steady herself by holding the furry
plush arms of the chair.

"We have always—shared everything," she said in a
low sad tone.

"I fully realize," he said earnestly, "that you and Miss
Mott have been in this house together a long time. That
you are very dear friends. But surely. . . ."

Lavinia stood up, so slight, so delicate that nobody
would even guess the strength in her fine bones. "She
would be lost without me," she said. "The years—the
sharing—how could I leave her alone now?"

"But surely someone else could come in and live with
her," he said.

A very small smile came onto her lips then. "It has
been arranged that I do the whipped potatoes," she said,

"While she does the table. It is too late to begin again, too late."

He could not move her, although he was desperately in earnest. He told her how lonely he had been, how much he needed her, how happy they would be . . . at that she flinched. He told her she had no duty beyond doing her best and was he worth nothing? He told her he had loved her from the first moment he saw her, and he told her God would bless their union.

But when he went away, Lavinia said goodby without giving him even a small hope. It was only after he had gone slowly down Maple Street that she collapsed on the steep stairway and sobbed so violently. And she began to talk aloud to the old hall tree, the dim portraits on the wall, and the pampas grass sent from Florida.

"She took me in, she made a home, we have shared too much too long. I cannot. I cannot."

She bathed her face and brushed her hair before Ella May got home.

"It was a fine meeting," said Ella May, "although I distrust that new Mrs. Bascom thoroughly. I think she has advanced ideas! My, am I tired. So nice of you to wait up for me. Is the milk hot?"

They sat at the kitchen table sipping hot milk with butter and a sprinkle of pepper in it. A traditional Mott affair.

"Now tomorrow it's your day to shop," said Ella May, "but may I suggest lamb? I notice it is cheap this week. And there are bargains in canned peas this week at Mr. Schreiber's."

Lavinia wrote down lamb and canned peas on a pad.

"Did you finish *Bleak House?*" asked Ella May.

"No."

"What a slow reader you are," commented Ella May. "I thought you were at the last chapter when I left. When I was in school, I was the fastest reader in my class, did I ever tell you that?"

"Yes, you did," said Lavinia.

She went upstairs and closed her door. They both had a feeling that a closed door prevented burglars. She looked around the little room; it was the back room, Ella May naturally had her mother's big front bedroom, and she saw the four-poster and the tufted spread and the dimity curtains and the woven rag rug. She went to the window and looked out, and the sky was very deep and splashed with stars.

She knelt and leaned her head on the clean white sill and cried bitterly and long, and the crying did not ease her; the tears boiled up in her eyes and fell down her face and she stifled the sound of her sobs so Ella May would not hear.

It was her turn to get breakfast in the morning, so she crept down and got the range going and made the pop-overs and fried the rosy country ham. And they ate, as they had always, at the table under the kitchen window. Ella May didn't notice that Lavinia ate almost nothing but drank two cups of tea.

When the postman blew his whistle, Lavinia got up—it was her turn—and brought in the *Christian Monthly* and the *Daily Crescent* and the laundry bill. And a letter addressed to her from Green Bend.

"What in the world is that?" asked Ella May, adding comb honey to her last popover.

"Well, dear me," said Lavinia, "Well! The Brewster house has been sold and the lawyer writes they found an old sign—the original old inn sign of great-great-grandfather—and would I care for it? Historic value."

"What in the world would you want an old sign for?" Ella May was practical.

"Why, I don't know," said Lavinia vaguely, turning the page. "It has a white deer on it and the name Thankful Brewster."

"How big is this thing?" Ella May's voice was a little sharp.

Lavinia was looking past her. "It's an antique," she mused, "the family name . . . grandfather's second wife took everything—stripped the house . . . we used to crack butternuts in the attic . . . it was leaning against the old chest then. . . ."

"Lavinia, you are not making any sense," said Ella May, "do you feel feverish?"

"I'll go over," said Lavinia, "the day you do the hospital. I'll go over and see," she repeated firmly.

"I don't see much use," said Ella May, "but you may as well go see. Might be something else there you'd want." She added, "I heard last night Reverend Mr. Sinclair will be leaving next week; the regular pastor is well again and the exchange is over. What a pity!"

"Yes, it is," said Lavinia softly.

The Reverend Mr. Sinclair did not appear at the library. He was presumably packing. Ella May and Lavinia planned the next turnout of the house and put up the tomato preserve as the tomatoes were richly ripe. They planned on how many jars they would need, and put them up accordingly. Ella May finished reading *Bleak House* aloud, and they did another bootee in pale blue.

And on the day Ella May did the flowers in the little

hospital, Lavinia drove over to see about the sign. They were having chicken pie for supper—Ella May did the chicken, Lavinia did the crust—and it was oven-ready when they both got home.

The little house was quiet and warm, the late sun laid a glory in the kitchen. The leaves were turning upside down and Ella May predicted a line storm. Big spongy clouds bucketed about on the horizon, so she sent Lavinia out to take in the cushions on the porch.

"It's always good to be prepared for anything," said Ella May. "Mother always said, better be safe than sorry."

Lavinia went out and looked up at the sky, a clear violet over the edge of the horizon but a darkish color near them. Clouds piled along the maples, as if they were beaten with egg whips.

"I hope he is at home," she said, carrying the cushions in and closing the door securely.

"But tell me about your trip," said Ella May briskly.

"I have the sign," said Lavinia breathlessly, "I have it. It's in the barn. I'll show you." She opened the door they had just shut, and ran out.

"Come back, Lavinia," Ella May called, "it might rain . . . feet wet. . . ."

Lavinia went into the barn, sweet with the musty smell of hay. She took up her sign, it was not really very large, and she ran back with it. The wind was rising; once she almost was whirled around backward, but she made it, and smiling, brought the treasure into the kitchen.

The sign was definitely antique; it had faded so the gilt scroll was a dim color, but the name of Thankful

Brewster was clearly legible and a gay white deer nibbled a pink posy underneath.

"There," said Lavinia, "isn't it wonderful?"

Ella May backed off.

"It's so nice and old," said Lavinia, wiping the dust from her fingers.

"It looks old all right," said Ella May, "covered with dirt and paint in terrible condition."

"I can clean it up," said Lavinia, "so nice of them to let me have it—it is truly valuable, he says, but I didn't have to pay a thing for it. Gave it to me so it could stay in the family. The white deer was from the Brewster coat of arms."

"Doesn't look much like a deer if you ask me," said Ella May coldly, "more like a horse."

"I think the date will come up," said Lavinia, "then it will be quite perfect."

"Who would ever want it?" asked Ella May. "An old disreputable thing like that?" She looked at it again. "What in the world," she said coldly, "do you expect to do with it, burn it for firewood?"

Lavinia put one hand on the sign. "Why," she said, in a faint voice, "why, I thought it was—it was so nice to have something from my family—from so far off—you see I never got anything on account of grandpapa's second marriage and all—I mean, no family pieces or silver—or anything. So I just thought this sign . . . well, it seemed very nice to have."

"I can't see what for," said Ella May.

Lavinia looked very shy all at once. "Well, I just thought," she said, hesitating, "that maybe we might—

well, we might put it on the barn—just put it there, just as a—as a sort of memento of my family."

Ella May bounced into the middle of the kitchen.

"Why, Lavinia, how ridiculous," she said, "how simply ridiculous! After all, my dear, this is a Mott house. This isn't a Brewster house! Certainly we couldn't put a Brewster sign on a Mott barn. What in the world made you think we could?" She added, with a little laugh, "Of course, you DO live here. But it is a Mott house!"

"I see," said Lavinia.

"If you want to keep it in the root cellar," offered Ella May, "we could move some jars and things."

"I don't think so," said Lavinia.

"Well," said Ella May, "you made a long trip for nothing, that's my opinion. Now it's your turn to get supper, but I have to go to the corner store for some bicarbonate of soda. So hold it up half an hour, will you?"

"Indeed you may have supper whenever it suits you," said Lavinia in a very odd voice, emphasizing the *you* markedly.

"Now don't get huffy," said Ella May briskly, "no reason to bother about a mouldy old board."

When the door closed behind her, Lavinia rushed upstairs to her room. This room, so peaceful, so secure, so settled, had a wild wind beating in the curtains.

Lavinia wrung her hands once, and once she sobbed out loud. But she stopped almost immediately. She had no time for tears.

She packed her bag, her best bag with the flowered carpeting sides. She put a few clothes, her white batiste night gown, her velveteen slippers, her ivory brush and comb, her curlers, her rice powder, in. She left the little clock Ella May had given her for Christmas and the Jerusalem beads (birthday from Ella May) which she had cherished. She pulled on a hat, the one with roses around the brim, found her white gloves. Flew down the stairs and took up the sign, leaning drunkenly against the table.

She ran out into the darkening world.

The black sky came down, the first big heavy drops fell. She bent her head and plunged into it, without even an umbrella or her rubbers. Or her mackintosh.

The rain was a wall of water. Her hat melted, her shoes squashed. The carryall banged her knees at every step and the sign clipped her smartly every few minutes as the wind caught it.

The last of the Brewsters and the only relic of the family went whacking along into the darkness and Lavinia was crying out loud to the windy gutters and whirling branches.

Suddenly she remembered that tomorrow was Tuesday and it was her day to polish the silver—the Mott silver. She set her lips and ran on.

The Reverend Mr. Sinclair was surprised when his brass knocker clanged. He was in the study off the Sunday School room of the church, as usual, working without much luck on his last sermon for the season. He had his shoes off, as his feet ached. He hurried to put them on and ran to open the door. Someone must be in trouble.

Wind and rain battled with the door, and on the step Lavinia and the carryall and the sign were almost swimming in water. She lifted her face, the soggy roses on her hat streamed extra water over her drenched face.

"Mr. Sinclair," she said in a pitiful voice, "may I come in?"

The Reverend Mr. Sinclair asked no questions. He was a man of God, but also a plain man. He scooped Lavinia up, sign and carryall and hat and all, and carried her in.

"Now, now," he said, "now, now, it is quite all right."

He loosed her fingers from the sign and laid the carryall on the walnut table.

"I have a little fire," he said, "come in."

Lavina stood up very straight and she did not look pretty at all, she looked a little like a Green Maenad.

"I must ask you," she said, in a tight whispering tone, "if you had—if you had—a—a family thing—from my family. . . ." She made a gesture toward the sign.

The Reverend Mr. Sinclair might not have been blamed for almost anything. For a maiden lady to turn up in the parson's study on a wild-storm night carrying Thankful Brewster banked by a white deer could well have made him recoil. Nothing in his ministerial experience could have prepared him for any such thing. And there was the carryall too.

But the Reverend Mr. Sinclair did not hesitate, not a fraction of a second.

"I should suggest," he said tenderly, "that over the mantel in one's home would be a most appropriate place for an historic item."

Quietly and in a ladylike manner, Lavinia fainted.

They were married in Winnetka, Illinois, by a schoolmate of Mr. Sinclair's. Lavinia took only enough time to buy a fresh lavender dress and a pair of slippers. Hers had shrunk so in the rain.

If she looked a little pale, it became her dark hair and darker eyes, and the minister's wife kissed her and blessed her.

When they moved from parish to parish, the Reverend Mr. Sinclair, grown portly and ruddy from Lavinia's excellent cooking, always made no bones about packing the sign with the rest of the luggage. Relic of my wife's family, he would explain; historic. She was a Brewster.

If he secretly thought the white deer resembled a horse remarkably, he never once said so.

In time, as he predicted, their union was blessed and two sons, although children of middle-aged parents, did very well, going to India and China as missionaries and having four children apiece.

Ella May said that Lavinia was always a little weak in her mind, that after all she had done for her, giving her a home, devoting herself . . . but one couldn't expect gratitude, could one? She never would understand what had possessed Lavinia to fly off in the worst storm of the year. . . .

She had forgotten the sign.

This should have ended the story, but it didn't.

For life has a way of keeping on happening.

In due course of time, the Reverend Mr. Sinclair died of lung fever, contracted when he went out in a blizzard to pray with an elderly parishioner.

Ella May Mott was gathered to her reward shortly thereafter from some unknown disease. She was buried in the Mott lot at the left side of the angel blowing the marble trumpet.

The Mott house came up for sale.

And was immediately bought, although nobody knew who had bought it until Miss Lavinia appeared with her trunks, a few boxes, and a rather large, flat package.

Lavinia moved quietly into the Mott house, disturbing nothing, changing no piece of furniture to another position. She tended it, carefully and gently, as Ella May would have wished.

She even kept up the garden, although she was no gardener, and the garden flourished. She could be seen in the long summer twilights with her garden hat pinned firmly to her still dark hair and her slender spare figure neatly garbed in a coverall and with her gloves on as she pruned the roses and weeded the delphinium.

The only change was a strange one.

Miss Lavinia had a sign put up between the front windows and back of the creaky porch swing.

It was an old sign, faded, but one could still see a white deer nibbling a pink posy, and still read the name, Thankful Brewster.

And, in time, all the neighbors called it the Mott-Brewster house!

Miss Fenella's Story

❊❊❊❊❊❊❊❊❊❊❊❊ ❊

Miss Fenella Worthington lived in a little white house on a dirt road that ran steeply from Green Bay Street to the Fox River. Our gang used to go by the house every day in summer on our way to the river to swim or go canoeing. Sometimes I had to stop with a pan of light rolls wrapped in a clean napkin, or a jellied veal loaf. Mamma was a great one for sending food to lonely people. "Poor Miss Fenella!" she said. "All by herself!"

"Why is she all by herself, Mamma?"

"Well, sometimes life doesn't quite work out the way you plan. Especially," said Mamma darkly, "for a woman."

Edie and Bill used to stop with me. There was a scraggly, untrimmed privet hedge, grown so tall it hid the yard and house. Behind it lay the garden, just a tangle of perennials—roses and lilacs and mock orange and delphinium. There was a Calycanthus bush by the porch, and when it bloomed we could pinch off a dark red-velvet flower and smell the exotic spice odor.

Inside, the house smelled of dried lavender. And dust. The parlor was a small, low-ceilinged room with too much big furniture in it. A rosewood piano and a harp took up one whole side. A dusty crystal chandelier hung in the center above the cream-colored carpet. There was a rosewood desk always covered with big sheets of writing paper. The chandelier didn't work, but there was a table lamp with a bronze base which depicted a colored boy eating grapes. The shade had long purple-silk fringe.

"I'm going to give the house a thorough cleaning," Miss Fenella always said, "as soon as I have finished my work. Turn it all out."

But she never did finish her work.

Edie and Bill and I would come in with our bathing suits over our shoulders and Mamma's present in a sweet-grass basket. Edie and I clumped in our big square shoes; but Bill, even then, walked quietly. In the elegant disorder of the parlor, Miss Fenella always was just rising from the desk.

The day I remember best was early June, much too cold for swimming but we were determined to try it. It was the good year for lilacs, and coming up to Miss Fenella's porch, their heavy scent was almost too exciting to bear.

"Come in, my dears," said Miss Fenella, rising from her desk. She wiped her penpoint with a flannel.

"Mamma thought you might taste her fresh strawberry jam," I said. "May I put it in the kitchen?"

Miss Fenella was small and thin, and her hair, which

was white as milk, was always in need of brushing. Her skin was transparent and her mouth, beautifully shaped, was without color. Except for her eyes, she would have been like a white bisque figure, but her eyes were a shining, brilliant blue. The only thing was, you never knew whether she focused them on you when she looked at you or was seeing something else a long way away.

"Oh, what a happy day to see you!" she cried in her breathless voice. "My dears, I have the most wonderful story!"

I went on to the kitchen and put the jam on the table. The kitchen wasn't much like ours. It never smelled of food cooking. The only food I ever saw was bread and a box of China tea and now and then an open bottle of milk. Mamma had a fresh pat of butter and six brown eggs and a slice of sugar-cured ham packed with the jam.

When I got back, Bill and Edie were sitting on the dusty sofa and Miss Fenella was shuffling her papers on the desk. Edie gave me a look. Trapped again, it said. She got up as I came and began edging backward to the door, but Bill sat quietly, watching Miss Fenella with his bright dark eyes.

"We'd like to hear it," he said.

Edie gave a faint moan.

"Now you tell me exactly what you think," she said, happily fluttering down among the papers. "I want honest criticism."

I sat down beside Bill.

Miss Fenella read her story. The June sun came in and laid a wash of gold over the dusty room and the elegant furniture and Miss Fenella. Once in a while she stopped reading and looked at us with her shining eyes and said,

"Now don't hesitate to tell me. . . . Often a writer can't judge everything from the viewpoint of the reader."

I listened intermittently between times of wondering whether the water would be too cold, or if we'd be too late to go on downriver, and if Bill was crazy over Edie or was I his first choice. It was hard to tell about Bill. I smelled the lilacs, and watched a white butterfly through the dusty panes.

Bill listened.

It was a story about a Russian princess with night-black hair and black eyes, who had a Cossack lover; there was a good deal of snow and sleigh bells jingling and the czar came into it somehow. I remember the lover said several times, "Ah, thou flower of my heart, fly with me over the steppes!"

But in the end they tried to fly, and were both killed by somebody who seemed to oppose their union. "To die together, to die with thee in my arms, my true beloved, is better than life," said the expiring Cossack.

When she had finished, Miss Fenella looked suddenly pale. She laid down the last paper and said softly, "How do you like it?"

"It—seems sort of sad," I said.

"Oh, but it isn't really sad," she protested. "They died together, you see!"

"Faithful to the end," said Bill suddenly.

"Yes, that's it! Exactly!"

Edie roused herself to say in an artificial tone, "It is just a wonderful story, Miss Fenella! I love to hear about places like Russia and all."

I made another encouraging comment, feeling very awkward, and Bill said, "I'd like to go there. And see what Russia is really like. I always wonder if the folks there are anything like us. Do you suppose they think like us? Or different?"

"Russians," said Miss Fenella definitely, "Russians are poetic. They have the Russian temperament."

Edie said, getting up, "We have to hurry. Thank you for reading your story to us. It was most kind." Edie was raised polite in an Episcopalian way.

"Are you going to publish it?" I asked.

"Well, of course, naturally," she said, her hands fluttering, "art shouldn't be—be—commercial. But one does feel at times the need of a—wider public."

We got away and ran down the hill to the river. We put on our bathing suits in the old boathouse. Edie was braiding her hair to wind around her head, so Bill and I sat on the bank with the water cool at our feet.

Bill said, "She never has got anything published."

"No," I said, "and I guess we three aren't much of a public. It's all she has."

"I wish she could," he said. "She keeps trying all the time. She tries so hard."

Edie came out, looking like a fashion plate with her pleated serge bloomers and the red swimming blouse. "If you ask me," she said scornfully, "she's just a crazy old woman."

"She is not," I said hotly. "She may be different, but she's a lovely, lovely person!"

Bill looked at me and then looked at Edie.

"Everybody in town knows she's crazy," said Edie, flinging up her head.

Bill stirred his long bare foot in the mud. "Sure," he said, "she's crazy because she keeps trying to be a writer.

But if she could do it, she'd be the town wonder. You just got to succeed; that's what it comes to."

I looked up and a gray gull was swooping downriver. I didn't know why, but I felt aching sad all at once.

That was the day Bill first kissed me. I'd been crazy over him since eighth grade, but this one day he fixed it so we walked home past Edie's house first, and then to mine. There was half a block on Alton Street then that had only wild bushes and scrub trees on it and "For Sale" signs. It was around dusk-dark, and when we turned the corner there wasn't a soul in sight.

Bill stopped by a blossoming lilac and pulled a spray of purple and stuck it down my neck. I laughed and looked at him and all at once he kissed me. His mouth was still cool from swimming, but I felt burning hot.

He said, "I guess I picked my girl now."

"Why, Bill?" I said. "Why?"

"Oh—something. Something today. Maybe it was Miss Fenella's story."

"You mean—I'm like that Russian princess?"

"Well, no. I hardly think anybody is." He had his hand on my arm. "But it was something about Miss Fenella that made me know."

After that, I couldn't do enough for Miss Fenella. I was always trying to think of extra things to take her, and I sat for hours listening to her tales.

There was the one about the Japanese girl and the English officer, complete with cherry blossoms and kimonos and fans. And one about the mysterious beauty from Castile and the bullfighter. There were lots of them, for Miss Fenella wrote constantly.

Once I met the postman at her gate, his arms full of

brown paper parcels, and he said, "She seems to get a lot of catalogues, Miss Fenella does."

I took them in and they were all addressed in her own fine, delicate handwriting. She came to the door with her face lighted up like the church altar for Easter, but when she saw what I had, the light went out. Her hands were trembling as she took the parcels and I said impulsively, "Oh, Miss Fenella, they're just too good, that's it."

She looked old and tired for a moment, her mouth drawn in and her shining eyes cloudy. Then she smiled at me and said, "Well, you know, my dear, that must be the difficulty. Or perhaps they aren't quite—quite exciting enough!"

"Oh, my," I said, "how could anything be more exciting? I mean with all that happens. . . ."

She hesitated and looked at me, and then said with a little rush, "My dear, would you like a cup of tea? I—I've been too hard at work to make anything by way of little cakes or sweet things—but. . . ."

"Why, yes, thank you," I heard myself saying.

We drank tea from transparent cups with little violets on them, and I told her Bill had been elected editor of our school magazine. He was going to earn money working nights for the *Crescent*, reporting school events, too. Bill was wonderful.

I told her about my new dress and white satin pumps. Then she read me a few pages of her newest story which was laid in Arabia. Of course, it was only a rough draft, she said, but I could get the idea.

I asked her how it ended, and she clasped her hands over her limp, frilled blouse and said, "He rides his horse over the cliff with her in his arms. You see, they couldn't give each other up." Then a little catch came in her voice and she looked at me with such a wistful glance and said, "I wonder if the editors realize that isn't such a sad ending. It—is a happy ending, really!"

While I was still feeling sorry for her, I happened to ask her about the harp. If she played it and if it was hard to learn.

"No, I don't play," she said, after a little silence. "It—doesn't belong to me. It belonged to someone else." She hopped up quickly. "May I freshen your tea?"

"Thank you, no. I must go home."

She followed me down the flagstone walk as if she hated to be left. But she waved gaily. "Come soon! I'll have the new story done. I know you'll like it best of all!"

At supper I asked Mamma, "Has Miss Fenella always lived in the little house?"

"Oh, no, she was brought up in the old Worthington house; it's the Woman's Club now. She only took the little house after. . . . Margie, you eat your lettuce now!"

I nibbled a leaf. "What happened to her family?"

"Her mother and father died," said Mamma firmly.

Mamma was always tight as new wallpaper about gossip, but I persisted. "What did they die of? Consumption?" That was the only adult disease I was familiar with. Grandfather had it.

"No," she said. "What does it matter? It was a long time ago." I thought she sounded evasive.

"Was Miss Fenella the only child, Mamma?"

Mamma laid down her fork. "No," she said. "She had a sister."

"What happened to her? What was her name? Was it a funny one like Fenella?"

"She was named Aurora—after Mrs. Robert Browning."

"Who was Mrs. Browning?"

"Robert Browning's wife," said Mamma, disposing of Elizabeth Barrett neatly.

"Well, what happened to her, Mamma?"

"I don't know what became of her in the end," said Mamma, "and if you don't stop pestering me with questions, you'll never get through supper before Bill comes."

Mamma set her lips together the way she did when she meant business. I knew I couldn't push her any further. But I thought about it. What did she mean by saying, "in the end"? Aurora couldn't have died, could she? But if she hadn't died, didn't she come to see Miss Fenella, or write to her? Or why didn't Miss Fenella say the harp was her sister's? It was almost as if she didn't want to mention her.

I talked it over with Bill. Bill said, "What I always noticed was that she never says what she did when she was young. You know how people that age always do."

"So they do," I answered, surprised.

Bill said, "I'm going through the paper files when I get a chance, and see if I can find out anything about the family. I want to know."

We were pretty busy with the football dances and rallies that fall and it was quite a while before we had an afternoon to go downriver and have a last wiener roast. We had a dozen wieners, big plump ones from Feitelbaum's, and a dozen big crusty buns, a pat of sweet butter, a big jar of mustard, and a half-dozen bananas.

We were going to build a fire and watch the sunset and eat our supper. Edie had long since passed out of the picture, now that Bill and I were going steady.

As we passed Miss Fenella's, Bill suddenly stopped and said, "Let's just say hello."

Most of the things in the garden had frosted, and the tangle of withering stalks gave the house a sad and lonely air. Miss Fenella called to us to come in when we knocked, and got up from the desk. I thought she looked sick. She had an old shawl over her shoulders, and her hair was falling down her neck. She was awfully thin.

I noticed a pile of big envelopes on the desk addressed to her in her delicate handwriting. Bill asked her right away about her work and she said with a kind of desperate candor, "I felt so sure the Arabian story was just what they wanted. . . ."

We stood there awkwardly a moment and then she said, "Do sit down! I would like to give you a—cup of tea! If it—it isn't too late?"

Bill gave me a funny look and said, "Look, we are going on a picnic. Why don't you come along?"

She actually got pink with excitement, and then she said, "Oh—I am afraid—I mean I couldn't be away from the house that long. I never do. I should love it, but. . . ."

"Why couldn't you?"

"Well, one never knows when someone—might come. And—just go away." She moved her hands. "But," she said, "it's my first invitation in—in a long time! It's so kind, so kind of you!"

"Well, then," said Bill, giving me another look, "why don't we have the picnic with you? It's going to be cold downriver, anyway."

Miss Fenella looked as if she had been presented with the public library, columns and all. She clasped and unclasped her hands and her eyes were shining under the delicate lids.

We had our picnic in the parlor. Bill got enough dead wood from the garden for a nice fire, and we let it burn down and did the weiners in an antique warming pan she had. Bill told her all about the mazagine and the newspaper reporting he was doing, and in between times he asked her little questions. Did she remember when the Masonic Hall was built? Did she remember the fire in the skating rink? How did the town happen to have the statues of Peace and Plenty in the park? Did she know who gave them?

Miss Fenella ate like a modest and cultured wolf. Wieners were her favorite meat and she hadn't had any for a long time, she said. The fresh rolls too, and the bananas. I remembered her empty kitchen, and Bill sat on the floor, sort of squinting his eyes up at her and pressing on her another bun with mustard.

Afterward she read us the Arabian story which she felt was the most thrilling she ever had written. It was thrilling. It had everything. Even poison. Blood and tears and broken hearts and pursuits and death. Swooning ladies and noble brave Arab chieftains.

Bill said, "I guess there are kind of special reasons some things get printed."

She said, "I—I have spent so much on postage—and it—it does count up, doesn't it?"

There was nothing for us to say. We sat there, watching her tired face, and suddenly my heart ached like a cavity in a front tooth.

We talked together until quite late, and when we left her, a cold dark wind walked the road.

Bill said violently, "Heck, the old rabbit is starving to death; that's what worries me." He walked so fast I had to skip to keep up. "What's the matter with this damned town? Church sending money to China and Africa and letting her starve under their noses! What's the matter with the Woman's Club, and the Ladies' Aid, and the County Relief Association?"

I said, "Bill, she'd die rather than go on the town."

"Well, she'll die then." He was furious. "I bet that's the first meal she's had in a week. Somebody ought to do something about it."

I said, "Mamma will do something."

"Sure, she will. Mine wouldn't. Mine would think I was nuts, too, hanging around a crazy old woman. By the way, honey, she's not so old. She's not more than fifty-five or so."

"Who told you that?"

"She did," he grinned smugly. "What you think I asked her all those time questions for?"

"Oh, Bill, you're smart!"

"You bet I am," he agreed pleasantly.

Mamma said, "You can't offer her public help. Not to Fenella Worthington. You can't go carrying church baskets to her."

"Well, why not a Worthington?" I asked, and Mamma said before she thought, "To the daughter of the founder of the match company?"

"Why, Mamma, if that's who she is, then why is she so poor?"

"Because she trusted a man," said Mamma. "She signed over every bit of her stock, every penny of it. Let that be a lesson to you."

"But you signed over your Stanley Steamer stock to Papa."

"That was different. Papa isn't a singer."

I stared at her.

"Now don't go gossiping around," Mamma said. "Whatever Miss Fenella has or hasn't, she has a right to her own grief. I'll talk to Mr. West and get her a load of coal before winter sets in. He can just deliver it and say he doesn't want to be paid until next summer. And we'll try to carry her a present of food once a week."

"Mamma, did she marry a singer?"

Mamma said, "If there's anything I hate it's a prying Paul. Someday when you're older, I'll tell you about it, but not now."

Of course, we were pretty much absorbed getting ready for the Walkaround and Bill put in so much time on the paper that they told him he could have a regular reporter's job as soon as he graduated in June. He said thanks, but he was going to the University first and take journalism and learn some other junk. Even then, Bill always knew just what he wanted and how to go after it.

Before we knew it, June had come. Bill kept on for the summer at the *Crescent*, but I went to the lake with the family. I went to say goodby to Miss Fenella, carrying all I could manage of food. We were closing the house, I said, and didn't want to throw out so much. There was a lot, all right.

Miss Fenella was sitting at her desk, as usual, but there were no papers on it. She had on a silk wrapper, very faded and old, and her hair was in braids. She had been crying.

I tried to pretend I didn't notice, so she made a great to-do over putting the food in the cupboard and being very bright and cheery. She followed me to the road, and then turned and gave me a lost, sad look as she said, "I'll miss you. But of course, I'll be terribly busy with my writing all the time."

"Of course, and I'll be home soon."

Then she clasped her hands and said softly and desperately, "The only thing is, I can't seem to think of anything exciting to write about! I . . . it's just a blank! And —one can never succeed if one doesn't keep working, can one?"

I said, "You need a vacation, that's it. Go out some."

"No, no! I didn't mean it. I only have a little headache —summer fever. I shall presently think of the most exciting new story. . . ." Her voice trailed away. She looked frightened.

I said, "I'll write you from Lake Kinnesec."

Her face lit up. "Oh—you will? I'll be able to get a letter from the postman? Oh, I haven't had one in—in—a long time!"

I was just getting over my first sunburn when Bill wrote. The main thing he said aside from the fact the town was a dead dump without me was that he'd found something out about Miss Fenella in the old newspaper files. In the church notes, it said Aurora Worthington had played a harp solo for the Easter musicale and Miss Fenella Worthington had sung *The Resurrection*.

So it was Aurora's harp. But what was the mystery about it? I wrote Bill that I thought perhaps the sisters had quarreled over the estate after their father and mother died. Bill wrote back triumphantly that he had found a whole column about the tragic death of the Worthingtons. They were trying to catch a train, he said in brief, and the horses were being driven as fast as possible when one of them got frightened and reared up and the carriage was overturned. Mrs. Worthington died immediately; Mr. Worthington lived a day in the hospital and expired. At his bedside were the two charming and beautiful daughters, Aurora and Fenella. Bill said, "Move over, Sherlock Holmes, here I come."

But he didn't find out anything more, except that the files of the paper were incomplete for that time and nobody seemed to know why.

We both went away to college that fall and I forgot all about Miss Fenella, although Mamma wrote once that the boatman had bought half of her lot to put a shack on, so Miss Fenella had a little money. Mamma called once and found Miss Fenella writing a novel. About the Scottish Highlands. She said dryly that the house could stand a good cleaning.

The next summer, Mamma and I visited our relatives in Spokane, a kind of preventive measure so Bill and I wouldn't insist on getting married before we were through school. Bill seemed to spend a lot of time swimming downriver and stopping in to see Miss Fenella.

He wrote that she was giving us a lace spread of hers when we got married. And he'd found out that the name of the singer was Estevan Olivares. There was a big pile of music he'd helped move out of the way once. Estevan's name was all over it in violet ink.

When even Spokane failed to quiet Bill and me, the family allowed us to announce our engagement. But we were to finish school and Papa wanted to know Bill's plans for the future.

"Why," said Bill, as if surprised anyone shouldn't know, "I'm going to be a writer!"

What the family said about that is neither here nor

there. If Bill had settled on raising rattlesnakes, it would have been better. Or wanted to starve to death on a government claim.

"I'll show 'em," he said. And maybe, at that, the family opposition helped him along, because that was why he wrote his novel for the University prize. They gave one every year for the best undergraduate novel, a thousand dollars cash and publication for the book.

The night before we went back to school, we said goodby to Miss Fenella. She had a cold and wore a rag around her neck. She was coughing and wheezing, but she was radiant at our news. Her blue eyes, rimmed with red, shone at Bill. "Love," she said, "is what living is for."

"Now how in heck does she know about love?" he puzzled.

I told Mamma about it. "Mamma, if she was married to Estevan Whatnot, why is she called Miss Fenella? Was she really married?"

"Yes, and no," said Mamma. She gave us a kind of ex-asperated look. "You two," she said, "have been mousing around that poor soul for years. Now you're old enough, I suppose I may as well tell you—just to keep you quiet. Yes, she was in love. He was a good-for-nothing fellow who came here to sing. He found out how much money the Worthingtons had, and began to court Fenella. She was eighteen." Mamma sighed. "She ran away with him and when her family tried to follow and prevent them getting married, they were killed on the way to the train. Both of them. But Fenella got back before her father died."

"But they were married?"

"Oh, yes, they were married long enough for the estate to be settled and Fenella to give it all to him for a silver mine in Mexico."

Bill was simply wolfing it down. "And then what?"

"Then," said Mamma, "he ran off with Aurora."

We couldn't get another thing out of her. But Bill really had something now. He kept going over it until he wore me down.

"She kept the harp," he said. "I think it's Aurora she expects to come back. Or else she'd sell it, poor as she is. Think of it," he said, "feeling she'd been responsible for her father and mother dying and then the man running off with her younger sister—and all these years she's lived in the little house with all those memories. Now I see why all her heroes are faithful forever and why they die in each other's arms."

When Bill won the prize and the book came out, he couldn't wait to get home and run down to Miss Fenella's. He seemed obsessed with anxiety and nervousness. By then it was full deep summer, August, and a haze lay over the road. Miss Fenella's house and land were going to be sold for nonpayment of taxes the next month, and it seemed to me you could feel a sorrowful air in the untended garden, even with the late roses spilling all over, sweet as spice.

Bill carried his book as if it were loaded with shotgun shells.

Miss Fenella didn't come to the door, or call. We went in anyway. There was no such thing as her not being home. But she was in bed, in the high, carved bed. She said she had a touch of summer fever. She looked flushed enough, but her hands were like a snow bank.

We sat down and I asked her about her work. She looked away, out of the dusty window, and said in a tired, thin voice, "My dear, I. . . . It has seemed to me lately that I—I may have been—mistaken." Her hands moved on the quilt. The word seemed so final, so sad, it echoed through the room, up to the cobwebs in the corner.

"I always hoped to—to give something to the world," she said in that faint voice. "One does want to. In a small way, of course."

Bill said roughly, "But you have, Miss Fenella! You have!" He reached over and laid the book on the bed. "This is my book."

Her hands fluttered over it, caressed it. "You wrote a book, Bill! A real book!" Her eyes shone. "It has a leather cover!" She turned it over and over. "And gilt edges," she said.

"I want you to read it."

"Read it to me," said Miss Fenella. Her eyes were on his face and her mouth was trembling. She said, "It's your turn to read to me now!"

Bill read. On and on, while the afternoon sun dipped the dust in gold and the scent of blown roses came in mingled with the smell of dried lavender.

It was all there, in Bill's book. The little town and the big mansion. The two girls and the harp and the delicate muslin frocks. The horses with sweat dark on their flanks. The fear and the anxiety and the death. Everything was there, changed by Bill's own feeling, but tangible and alive.

It took a long time, and Miss Fenella never moved once. The room was filled with dusk by the time Bill finished. The room was filled with the drama and excitement and suffering and wonder that goes on in the heart in a little place among little people.

Bill put down the book finally. There was a silence, a kind of tight silence. My head was aching. My stomach was in knots. Bill looked pale and his mouth had little drops of sweat on the upper lip.

Then Miss Fenella spoke. She said, "Why, Bill—why, Bill—that's my story!"—and her voice was like crystal.

Bill wiped his face. "Yes," he said, "it is. Yours and mine."

"In a book," she said, with wonder. "In a real book, with gilt edges!"

Bill went to the window and looked out and I knew he was crying and not wanting to. He said, in a strange voice, "You . . . it's all right?"

"I've collaborated," she said, sinking back on the pillow. "I've collaborated with you!"

Bill came over then and said, almost angrily, "Yes, and you're responsible for that book! You see? You see?"

A bee stumbled against the pane and was too loud.

She said, "But, Bill, it was a blue dress she wore that day, not gray. It had ruffles around the hem. She was—she was much more lovely than I ever . . . even though she was—headstrong. It had a sash of pale yellow."

Bill looked at me.

"Well, if the rest is all right," he said, with a heavy sigh.

"It wasn't Aurora's fault," she said. "Nobody could help it. He—he was—so romantic!"

"I know," he said. "I know."

He got up and leaned over the bed.

"It's your book," he told her. "I just sort of copied it down from being around with you. So you've really succeeded, you see." He smiled. "I learned all about how to write from you!"

Somebody was banging on the front door and that broke up the breathless moment. We went out and the town taxi was still pouring hot smoke over the desolate garden. A plump woman was picking her way across the flagstones. She said, "I am looking for Miss Fenella Worthington."

I said, "She's ill, in bed. Shall I see if? . . ."

"Thank you, I'll go right in."

She hopped up the steps. We walked on, down the dusty road, where the twilight was just falling in a soft violet light.

"Bill," I said, "whoever in the world was that?"

He gave me a look that was full of pity.

"That was Aurora," he told me. "She's come back. I knew she would."

"Bill," I said, "how do you know? Maybe it was someone trying to sell something."

"I love you," he said. "You're a darling. But you never would make a writer."

"What does make a writer?" I asked. "And why didn't Miss Fenella ever write her own story that was so dramatic instead of all that Russian and Arabian junk?"

"Lord knows," he said. "Lord knows."

We walked on. Dust rose behind us. The sky was pale peach and the sound of the dam was soft thunder downriver.

Little Goat
Goes Up

❁❁❁❁❁❁❁❁❁❁❁   ❁

"Now look out, girl, you'll squash 'em," said George. "What do you think you are, Mary? Let 'em breathe."

The Lady Manitou Undaunted, known privately as Mary, rolled over on her back, held four golden paws in air. She stretched out her chin, presenting a soft silky place to be rubbed.

"Nice little gang you got here." George's brown steady hand rubbed comfortably.

Mary twiddled her brief cocker tail. Her long dark-golden ears lay limp on the pillow. She rolled an onyx eye at George, and said pleasantly, "Glumph."

Faint snufflings came from beneath her. A damp button nose pushed out, a tiny raspberry paw poked up under her left ear, a mouse noise sounded. George retrieved a satiny morsel, flipped up a second, shoved Mary aside, and counted the family.

Louisa bent over the box with him; her amber hair was the color of the nearest puppy, her blue eyes were shining, her mouth soft.

"Oh, the darlings," she said; then, "George, dear, don't you think Mary looks a little peaked?"

The Lady Manitou Undaunted kissed Louisa's nose happily.

"She's all right," said George, "she's got what it takes."

There were five puppies, wiggling, warm, soft, eager cocker children, three black-and-white males, husky and big pawed, a neat little golden girl, and the runt, black-and-white, also a girl.

"Of course that fifth one was just a mistake on her part," said George. "Four is plenty for any cocker to raise. No wonder the fifth is a poor specimen. Nobody could have five champions at once."

"Anyhow, we have four perfect beauties." Louisa gathered up a handful, set them carefully on the living-room table.

"Look at the bone on Toots here!" George lifted a paw, half-thimble size. Toots looked smug. Louisa posed the fat little body, chanting, "And the best of breed at the Specialty show was Manitou Magnificent, sired by Champion Swift Storm, out of Manitou Undaunted. We predict a brilliant future for this newcomer! Good luck to the young breeders, Mr. and Mrs. Stockton."

Mary got up and left the box, remembering suddenly the veal knuckle she had buried under the Persian rug. The four on the table rolled and whisked their tongues in and out and made snufflings.

The little runt lay alone on the pillow, shivering. She got up slowly, and wavered to the edge of the box, lifted a wrinkled muzzle to look eagerly at the two humans. Standing on weak hind legs, she tried to bounce over the edge. Falling back, she hit her nose violently. She got up again, and painfully jumped at the bars again. She whimpered softly. But nobody paid any attention.

George and Louisa were giving the others a special pinch of irradiated yeast. Mary was going over her bone to be sure it was aging well.

"Might as well give the runt some too," said George. "What do you want to do with her, Louisa?"

"We'll have to give her to somebody for a pet," Louisa said, "the poor little thing, she can't help being no good. But of course we can't have a poor one around—here, stop it. She's chewing the pillow."

George said seriously, "You've got to make up your mind to keep only the best, darling, if you really want to raise champions." He smoothed the runt's thin back. "She's just nothing but a little goat, poor little thing."

They went away. Mary got back in the box. The four upstanding offspring jammed the weakling away from the warm sweet milk. Her mother's hind leg nearly strangled the runt's throat, one eye was squashed shut by Toot's milky paw; with the other she looked out at a cold and difficult world.

If George and Louisa hadn't helped her out, she would have died; she always got what the others left. When they fell back, stomachs tight as drums, paws lax, she crept up for her thin lunch. But now and then, Louisa spooned something yellow and warm into her throat. She lived, precariously, but she lived.

She learned to amuse herself. She chewed. While George and Louisa posed and brushed and combed the others, she solaced herself with the hooked rug, or a tapestry pillow, or the edge of the kitchen linoleum.

"Dumb as a goat," said George. "Look at my best shoes! Simply riddled!"

"I don't mind that so much," commented Louisa.

"Naturally not, they are—or were—my shoes!"

"Well, look at the sleeve of my best pajamas! And last week she ate those two theater tickets and my last five dollar bill and my Irish Sweepstakes chance!"

"Can't teach her a thing. For Heaven's sake, let's give her to somebody."

"I guess we'll have to. I'm nearly crazy looking after the rest, let alone Little Goat."

Little Goat was spanked with a folded newspaper. She was shut up in the kitchen, where she took the enamel off the ivory table. She was tied in the dining room, and ate the middle out of the rug. She took the beatings with the same air of passive endurance that she had developed in the puppy box. It was just that kind of a world.

Toots bit her ear every time she got near him. Mary gave over family cares entirely, and snarled whenever Little Goat came close. Summer Storm and Cream Tart took the squeak mice and rubber bones. Little Goat's rather wide-set eyes watched the lamb-chop bones with the extra tail juicy on the end go to Toots, while her mouth dripped.

"Never give a dog a chop bone," said Louisa, handing one to Magnificent.

Then Little Goat began going away to strange places. The first place smelled of leather and warm plush. She was there a week, utterly lost and miserable, constantly

yelled at by a big smoky man. Then she was brought
back in disgrace, dumped onto the family pillow.

"She utterly destroyed six hundred dollars' worth of
antique tapestry," said a tearful voice. "I thought you
said, Louisa, that spaniels didn't chew things up like
terriers!"

She was dragged away again, and came back in four
days. She got used to being whisked off in a strange car,
stuck down in a new place, and brought back mysteri-
ously to a desperate Louisa.

Nobody wanted her. Things were that way.

She was at home, after one of these trips, when the
big dog-show season began. Lying under a chair with
her nose wistfully sticking out, she watched George and
Louisa clipping and combing and brushing the indolent
Toots and the sleek golden girl, Cream Tart. Dark-
golden curls sifted over Louisa's blue smock; George was
red and earnest. They all had special food.

"And darling, if we should win a small cash prize,"
said Louisa, "you're going to have a brand new hat! One
of those flattish Esquire things."

"Got to have a moustache for that," grinned George.
"Look, baby, should I take a shade off under her ear?"

Finally one day they went off, all of them, and left
Little Goat alone. She padded around the house, nose
intent. She got hungry, ate two book covers and a string
of beads. Then she crept onto the pillow and dozed, hearing the silence creak in the walls.

Toots came back with a blue ribbon, shining, resplend-
ent. Cream Tart had a pink one. George and Louisa were
very happy. There was steak for supper, browned in butter. Manitou got the bone. Still it was very nice to have

them back, until Louisa saw the books and missed the beads.

"I've had all I can stand," she wept. "Oh, you wretched Little Goat, my only good beads! I wish you'd never been born."

Little Goat crept under the sofa. She lay very flat in the darkest spot. Her unbrushed ears gathered a film of dust. Her tail was not merry. When she was dragged out and started on another trip, this time in a box, she didn't even chew the slats. The box was dark and smelly and a thunderous roar went with it. She lay taut, eyes glazed. Finally the roar ceased, she was pulled out of the darkness, the light dazzled her.

She was in the country. A man in brown stood beside her, wiping his greasy hands on his overalls. A couple of strange shaggy dogs glared at her from the porch steps.

"Come here, Mamma," called the man. "The spaniel's here, the one they have to get rid of."

Little Goat sat still, waiting for whatever was coming to her.

A woman in an apron swung the screen door, and came out. "My goodness, what a puny little mite," she said. "You going to board her, Jim?"

"Just till they can sell her," he nodded. "Guess I'll shut her in the run."

Little Goat was stiff. She got to her feet and wabbled a little, still dizzy. Then a new scent pricked her nose, a rich, heady smell. Her heart gave a hard slow thump. She lifted her muzzle, sucked in the air. There—there—she found it! It came from a tall feathered thing walking in the grass far away. Her mouth was wet.

There was something special to do. She quivered. She

gathered her paws together and leaped like a streak across the grass. Her ears flopped, her muzzle was low. The thing rose with a squawk. Instantly, Little Goat dropped flat to the grass, rigid, nose flat. She had to do it. The man shouted. She quivered, lay motionless. It was in her to lie still when this happened.

Then there would be another folded newspaper, she would be wrong again.

But there wasn't.

The man came over, his hand came down, touched her gently. "My God, I believe she's a natural," he said. "Mamma, did you see her flush and drop, and hold it? And not a day of training, I know."

"Well, let's give her a good meal," said Mamma, "before you get her in the field."

The big shaggy dogs resented her. They said so. They continued to resent her all summer as she ran behind them, tongue out, breath laboring in her small lungs, her city-feet sore and bleeding. When the man wasn't around, they snapped at her. But she minded her own business. She slept in the barn on a pile of hay, she ate raw meat, her coat was thick with burrs, but now and then the man put his hand on her head, after a hard day, and said, "Not such a dumb goat after all."

When the leaves turned red and yellow and the nights frosty, her fur had thickened. Her ears hung to the ground, her brisket was covered with heavy curls, her straight legs were heavily fringed, muscles rippled close over her shoulders.

She was in the front yard keeping a wary eye on the white hens when the postman came with a letter for the man. He read it on the steps, pipe in his teeth.

"Mamma, come out!"

Mamma came out, sat beside him.

"They're selling Little Goat," he said.

Little Goat pricked up her ears. Her tail twiddled.

"They got an offer from a kennel for twenty-five dollars. For a brood matron with the Undaunted line. My God, I'd keep her myself if I had it."

Mamma said, "Jim, you can have my egg money."

He set his mouth. "I don't dare. Mamma, we have that mortgage payment the fifteenth. We're short a hundred dollars. I—I haven't been able to borrow a cent!"

They sat there, not saying anything. Little Goat moved up, sat on the bottom step.

"What will we do, Mamma?" the man cried suddenly. "This time it was the corn borers. I don't know where to turn."

Mamma got up. "Well," she said quietly, "twenty-five dollars won't save us." She went into the house, came out again with the cracked teapot. "You send Louisa and George a check for Little Goat," she said, "and then you enter her in the field trials. Just like you wanted to."

"But she's just a novice. Never been in a trial."

"All these days you've worked with her," said Mamma, "now you've got to take a chance on her. She might—she just might—win the fifty novice stake."

The man bent down, lifted Little Goat's head, stared into her wide soft eyes. "You wouldn't let me down, would you, old girl?"

Little Goat looked back. Her tail moved.

"There'll be worse dogs than her skiting after those pheasants," he said thoughtfully, "but Mamma, the competition is killing in this trial. On account of the two-hundred-and-fifty-dollar grand prize the state club is offering. And if I take your egg money. . . ."

"Go along," said Mamma, "where's your gumption, Jim?"

He stood up, squared his shoulders. "All right, I'll chance it!" he said.

There came a week of terrible work. And no tidbits, just one meal of lean beef at night before she crawled thankfully to the pile of hay. Then another racketing journey, this time in a little old car, with the shaggy dogs riding large and insolent in the tonneau, and Little Goat snicked into a corner in front between Mamma and Jim.

Little Goat was sick. She rested her head on the hard guncase and closed her eyes and was sick. Her mouth dripped, her nose burned, her stomach heaved. But she made no sound. She knew better. After an endless time, the car jolted to a stop, Mamma and the shaggy ones tumbled out, a box was opened, Mamma offered her a meat cake, Little Goat turned away her head. The shaggy ones lolloped it up. They went on.

After a timeless interval, the car stopped again and they all got out, dragging Little Goat with them.

She looked up with her wide eyes, and saw a hill, brown and cold, swarming with people. A group of men in boots and leather coats stood at the hill's edge, cradling guns. Little Goat knew all about guns now. Other men had dogs on leashes, dogs like her, and dogs like the shaggy ones.

"Springers over this way!" called one of the men, and the man whistled the shaggy ones over.

"Oh, look at the sweet little cockers," cried a girl, running past Little Goat.

Little Goat sat down on her haunches, patient. This was hunting, but strange hunting. Three men passed carrying large gunny sacks, heavy on their shoulders, and the sacks smelled deliciously of pheasant. Three girls in red coats came up and stuck pointed things in the ground and sat on them. "Why don't they begin?" said one. "It's simply freezing out here!"

Jim came back. "The course lies down to the valley and up the other slope," he said. "God, it is a tough one. It's all briars or heavy swamp. The springers are first; I'm taking Bessie out now. We're off soon as the guns are lined up." He wiped his face; he was red. Bessie strained at her leash.

Little Goat trembled, tugged at her own leash. "No, you sit still," said Mamma. "I ain't going to drag myself around in those briars. We'll just set right here, you and me. I can see all I want."

Well, that was the way it was. Little Goat sat up, saw all she could. Nobody noticed her. A tall thin man read loudly from a paper. "The gallery is requested to stay back," he said.

The men dropped over the hill in pairs, the handler and his dog leashed, the official Gun ahead. Leashes slipped, the dogs began to move ahead. Somewhere a shot popped the sudden stillness, the gallery swarmed away, Little Goat couldn't see any more. Her muzzle quivered. If she just could see over that hill!

Occasionally shots boomed, followed by faint cheering. She was always out of it. She bit a dead blade of grass; her mouth was watering. The wind brought smells. Smells of woodsmoke, bitter, tangy. Smell of crushed dry grasses, of gunpowder, of bird. Possibly rabbit, also. Wild rich smells meant to be tracked. She couldn't help it, she whimpered.

At noon they all straggled back, men and girls and guns and dogs. They drank out of bottles, and laughed. More people kept driving up, dogs were everywhere. Jim was pretty sober. "Bessie got fouled," he said, "and Ginger didn't raise a bird."

Mamma said, "Drink your coffee, Jim. Never mind."

He put his hand over his eyes, "But we need the money so damned much, Mamma. Guess I'm not much of a trainer after all."

Mamma said sturdily, "You do the best you can, that's all right."

"The official Guns are ninnies," said Jim. "I never saw worse shots. They're putting down fresh pheasants. Look yonder, Mamma, there's the springer champion, Man O'War. It's a walkaway for him. He'll have the two-hundred-and-fifty by six o'clock. Well, that's that. You getting cold?"

"Guess I'll go back to the car a while," agreed Mamma.

She sat in the car with the windows closed. Little Goat couldn't see anything. She found an old pasteboard box and ate it. She hurt inside. She dozed drearily. When the man came back at last, she didn't even look up.

"Get out, Little Goat!" his hand was on her. "It's your chance. Your first—and last hunt!"

Little Goat trotted after him, ears swinging. She began to tremble. The man pulled her to the brow of the hill. His hand was on her again. "Take it steady, old girl. Don't forget the rules," he said. "Watch my hand for direction, and never, never let go when you get your bird. Remember!"

"Ready?"

"We're off!"

The leash slipped. Little Goat drew a lungful of air, swung over the hill. There were too many people, too many dogs, she wanted to run and run, away and away. "Steady," said Jim's voice. She jerked herself back. Dropped her muzzle, and began to quarter her field. This was business. She turned to take direction from Jim. He never spoke, he waved his hand, she trotted over the field, her nose was busy.

This was queer hunting. Sometimes he wouldn't let her go on a scent, sometimes the gun missed, and the pheasant flew away happily, while Little Goat stared. Once when she covered a bayberry patch and allowed it to be empty, she was called in, and another dog sent over the place. Anger rose in her. Hadn't she just said it was empty? But the other dog failed to flush anything, and a man wrote some marks down on a paper. The day wore on, it was all confusing, and she was tired. Her tongue lolled, burrs matted her coat, a briar ripped her nose. But when it was ended, Jim laid his hand on her and grinned. "Good girl."

It was the first time she had been praised. She had a funny feeling. She lifted her eyes, looked up, tail whirring.

She trudged along, leashed, while Champion Man O'War did his stuff. The gallery cheered him wildly, he flashed back and forth, dropped expertly to hand, retrieved to the handler's glove. It was smooth hunting, expert, finished.

"There's one more bird at the edge of the course," said

the judge, "didn't mean to plant it there, but it got away."

"All right, I'll get my dog to bring it in." Man O'War swung away again, flicking a lordly ear.

They all scrambled after, through a tangle of vines, across a bayberry thicket, through a wood of young juniper and pine, past a swamp. The gallery halted on the last rise of ground; the going was terrible. Little Goat felt the soreness in her pads as she scrubbed through wild raspberry.

Sun slanted over the covert, Man O'War advanced majestically. He pushed into the thicket. It was a piece of low ground, dense with briar, thorn, blackberry, and raspberry. Man O'War ran back and forth in front of it, he thrust his big shoulders against unyielding masses of briar, he backed out, pushed in again.

There wasn't room for a rabbit. He sat down, looked back at his handler.

"Get in there!" shouted the man. His face was red.

Man O'War got up and flung himself at the dense growth again. Branches snapped. He wormed his way in a few feet, then slowly he backed out and lay down. He was through, he knew what was possible and what wasn't. He licked a torn paw.

"Well, we'll have to let that one go," said the judge. "It can't be done. Unless somebody else wants to try." He laughed. "Any dog gets there walks home with the $250. Otherwise, it goes to to Man O'War on his performance."

Little Goat tugged at the leash. She whimpered. She snapped her teeth together. She jumped up against the man, her eyes big, dark.

"You can't get in there," he said. "Come on back, it's impossible."

Little Goat whimpered, strained.

The man stared an instant. Slipped the leash. "Let my bitch have a try," he said shortly.

"Well, if you want to. . . ." the judge shrugged.

"Go, then," said Jim. "Do it, old girl. Do your best!"

Little Goat went in.

Lying on her belly, she crawled over the rough ground, muzzle down, thorns raking her compact body. The close net of branches closed her in, the light dimmed, a thorn ripped her eyelid and a trickle of blood soaked down her lip. Berry prickers whipped her legs, more painful than the old folded newspaper.

But she smelled bird, wild, fresh, gamey. And Jim had said, "GO." Her nose quivered. She shook her head to clear her sight, crawled again, dragging her ears against the punishing needles.

Inch by inch, she pushed in deeper and deeper, her shoulders heavy against the drag of thicket, one eye swelled completely shut.

But there she caught it again, the smell of pheasant; she moved toward it. She crashed through laced briars, ears torn ragged, and there was a whir of brilliant wings as the pheasant, flushed, rose sharply in the air.

Little Goat dropped flat, muzzle steady, though nobody could see her in that dense mass.

There was the ping of a gun, the pheasant wheeled in air, came down, and flew up again. Little Goat rolled her one clear eye balefully back in the direction of the poor shooting. The bird, winged, flew dizzily, came down again, deeper in the tangle.

So Little Goat began all over, following the scent which came thin in the dank air. Twisting and turning, scratched and torn, both front paws split open, she wormed her way ahead. It was harder than ever to see, but she strained ahead, made a desperate thrust with her shoulders, flushed the bird again, waited, her heart laboring, for the shot.

The gun missed again. She licked the fine slobber from her lips, gave a snort of disgust, but the pheasant wheeled down again, beating one helpless wing.

The bird, she had to get the bird. Bring it in.

She flung her weary body against those maddening thorns and ripped through, shaking blood from her eyes. The bird, down, was on the ground, struggling in a briar bush. It tried once to rise, flopped over, beat its wings helplessly.

Little Goat thrust her soft muzzle straight into the briar and took it, getting a bad hold because of the bush, but bringing it out.

She braced her feet, lifted her head, backed away, and turned painfully toward the distant gun.

The pheasant, fluttering, spread out its good wing. Little Goat's eyes were covered completely by a feather screen. Of course she couldn't drop the bird for a better hold, that was absolutely against the rules. Never, never drop your bird. There was nothing for it but to smell her way back in the darkness, inch by inch, a dragging desperate struggle; she no longer thought about getting back, she just crawled on, paw after paw.

She fell down, ran blind into a stump, was fouled by a length of rusty barbed wire frome some old fence. The barbs stripped her left hind leg open, paralyzed the muscle.

Now she heard the man's voice, calling her in. She might drop the bird and make it. He was calling her. She sank onto her belly for a dizzy moment, her legs weren't working right. Then she got up, and fumbled ahead. Never drop your bird. Never drop your bird.

Little Goat came out from the thicket with the bird.

She couldn't see anything, with the spread wing over her eyes. The people stood still. There wasn't a breath. She dragged herself over the ground, smelling for the man. In that curious stillness she pulled herself over the rough ground until she staggered to his feet. Then she laid down the pheasant, and laid herself down beside it.

A great shout went up. Little Goat wondered dimly why the people were so noisy. She heard the roar of voices, she heard the judge, hands clapped loudly, and in a still louder burst of applause, Jim stepped forward and took something in his hand that crackled.

"Thank you, sir," he said. "You don't know what this means to me. It's. . . . Thank you, sir."

He stood over her, the pheasant, still alive, in his hand. Then Little Goat heard another voice, a voice that she knew. Louisa's voice.

Painfully she opened her good eye, tried to move her tail. Louisa flew to her.

"Little Goat, Little Goat," Louisa was sobbing. Her soft clean cheek came down to Little Goat's dirty bloody head.

There was George. The hand he put on her was shaking. "Great old girl, wonderful old girl," he said.

Her head was confused, a film came over her eye.

When it cleared, she heard Jim saying, "I wouldn't sell her back to you. After all, she's really your dog. The transfer papers aren't even signed. I—I wouldn't feel like I could take advantage of you. Just because she's such a—such a winner."

And George said, "Jim, if you let us keep her—I—I well, I can't tell you—you know how it is with us, just getting started and all—how would it be if I add fifty to the prize money—for your training—would that be any help to you?"

Jim said, "Help? It'll mean Mamma and I can pay the mortgage this week." He grinned, "Little Goat has saved the place."

Little Goat was carried to the car in Louisa's arms. Toots was waiting in the front seat, shining, immaculate, smug. Manitou Undaunted lolled in the back seat.

"Get over, Mary," said George, giving her a push, "make room for your betters. Better put her down, Louisa, she's bleeding all over your brand-new fur."

Louisa got in, holding Little Goat. "She wants to sit in my lap," she said. "Oh, George, the poor darling!"

"Oh, she'll be all right," said George, starting the motor. "Little Goat can take it, all right."

"Are you by any chance," inquired Louisa, "speaking of Manitou Miracle Maid, the field trial champion?"

Little Goat snuggled in Louisa's arms. Louisa smelled sweet, she was warm. Her hands were rubbing the tired places.

Little Goat laid her head on Louisa's shoulder and began to chew out large hunks of Louisa's fox fur. It was a pretty swell world. That was the way it was.